One Dirty Table

G. Burke Morrill

One Dirty Table
©2023 G. Burke Morrill

All rights reserved. This book or any portion thereof may not be reproduced or used in any manner whatsoever without the express written permission of the publisher except for the use of brief quotations in a book review.

print ISBN: 979-8-35093-850-0
ebook ISBN: 979-8-35093-851-7

for Gloria

CHAPTER ONE

The morning sang softly in D minor. My eyes were full of dew and lack of sleep. I knocked. A long moment later the door creaked open. Her mother stood on the other side. She looked old—the soft curves of her face stretched tight, her shoulders held forward. Her eyes—the same as her daughter's—jade with a corona of amber—eyes that had been stark in contrast to everything, now faded into the rest of her like those of an apparition.

"Can I help you?" she said, lowering her gaze to the rough wooden boards beneath my feet.

"It's me, Mrs. Scott. It's George. George Muirhill."

She brought her eyes up slowly and let them fall upon my face. She reached out her left arm as if to touch my cheek, but pulled her hand back at the last moment, almost as though she expected me to fade away. "George," she said. "It is you isn't it? You look so grown up..." The hint of a smile formed on her lips, but never touched her eyes. "Well, come inside...please...I'll get you some tea."

Although memory told me that the Scott's living room looked just as it had so many years ago—the same blue couch, the same pictures hanging ever so crooked on the wall, the same red lamp that sat on a wicker end table just outside of the door to the kitchen—the feeling of the place was foreign now: A movie set wrenched from my past.

"Have a seat," she said, motioning to her kitchen table. I watched her walk slowly to the refrigerator, her slippered feet barely coming off the floor with each step, pull out a bulbous pitcher painted with blue and yellow birds, and pour tea from it into two matching glasses. "I don't know where she is," she said calmly as she sat down across from me. "The last time she called was almost a year ago. I've left messages." Tears began falling silently onto her slate-gray blouse. Over the past few months, the color gray had enveloped everything around me—as if there had been no Oz at all.

Mrs. Scott rose from her seat and walked towards me, her bony fingers grasping still my nearly full glass. "I'll get you some more tea." When she returned to the table, neither of us touched our glasses. I watched mine. Watched one round bead of condensation form slowly and then run down the glass and into the red-brown wood. It occurred to me in one of those sideways thoughts that sprout from trying too hard to focus, that I had never seen a glass on Mrs. Scott's table without a coaster. I stood up and walked over to the island in the middle of the kitchen and slid open the drawer on the far left side. The tray of coasters, stacked neatly in two rows of three, was exactly where it had been over twenty years ago. I pulled out two, each white with dark green vines forming a twisting border on all four sides.

She again stood up and walked slowly over to the granite countertop on the opposite side of the room. My father had replaced the warped vinyl that had come with the house with the polished gray rock speckled with black and white flecks. She lifted the lid of a blue letter box and pulled out a folded piece of paper, walked back over to me, and placed it on the table next to my left hand. "That's the one she called from. I don't know what you can do with it." She turned away. "I think you'd better go now, George," she said. "If you see her—" She stopped and looked out the window, into the brightness of the day. Her face fell, as if, in remembering one moment from the past out of which I suppose I had emerged, she'd finally made her mind up about something else. By the time I realized I had forgotten to thank her, she was halfway to the living room, whispering regards to my mother. I stood in silence until I heard the door to her bedroom click firmly shut.

I pulled the front door behind me gently, the folded piece of paper cupped in my hand having turned to lead. For the first time in months I removed the two glass T-top sections of the roof of my car, rolled down the windows, and let the wind wash over me as I held the pedal beneath my foot firmly against the floor. Flashing blue lights jerked me out of my head less than five minutes later. I pulled over to the shoulder and watched the cop get out of his car and walk slowly towards my side mirror. He was short and muscular. His uniform, stretched tight. He strode towards me like that asshole at a bar you could tell was looking for a fight. He wore sunglasses—the kind with big, silver lenses that hid his eyes. As he peered into my window I could see two of myself reflected back.

"Do you know how fast you were going!" he said to me vehemently. My eyes darted from his glasses to the throbbing vein on the left side of his neck.

"No," I said dryly after a moment's pause, "I don't."

"George! George Muirhill? Is that you!"

"Yeah," I said as I looked back up at him.

"It's me, George. It's Franklin, Franklin Paz! Man it's been a long time. How are you? When did you get back to town? Why were you going so fast?" he enthusiastically rapid fired at me.

"Franklin?" I said, as I tried to create in my mind the transition from Franklin Paz as I knew him—a short, round gadfly—to the confident, strong man I faced today. "Yeah…I just had to get out of town."

"Out of town? George, when did you get back?"

"Yesterday."

"Why are you leaving so soon?" I just stared back. "Well, you're lucky I'm the one who pulled you over. Hey, I tell ya what. I won't take you to jail for going seventy in a thirty-five, and you'll come grab somethin' to eat with me and catch up. Sound good?" His smile was the same.

"Yeah. Sounds good."

Franklin was married now. He had a son—a five-year old—Arthur. After high school he enrolled in the police academy and then joined the small department here in town. His father had left when Franklin was ten. He told me that morning, sitting in a corner booth of Ruth-Ann's diner—two scrambled eggs, sliced cantaloupe, and turkey sausage in front of him; French toast drowned in butter and syrup on the burnt orange table top in front of me—that he could never leave. He had been offered opportunities—promotions—but they all required him to move. Pensdale was his home, he said.

I asked him about Liberty as our plates were cleared from the table, but he hadn't heard anything. He asked to see the number that Mrs. Scott had given me. "This is an Atlanta area code, George," he said with smiling eyes.

"Okay."

"You should go there. See if you can find her."

"Yeah, maybe."

"I've looked for you online, George. You and Liberty. Are you not on it?"

"On what?"

"Online. Why not, George? Don't you want to see what's going on with all the people you grew up with?"

"No."

"No? George—" he began again enthusiastically.

"Here," I said, cutting him off as I tore a corner from the unfolded piece of paper and scribbled down my cell. "Now we can stay in touch."

Yeah, thanks!" he said, beaming. "You should really go to Atlanta. You should go and try to find her. Who knows, maybe you'll run into her as soon as you get there."

"I don't know. Maybe. It was good seeing you, Franklin."

"Yeah, you too George. I'm gonna call."

"I know." We both got up from the table and shook hands.

"I gotta go, George. Talk to you soon," he said as he walked away. When he reached the door, he stopped and turned around. "Slow down. Ok?" he said smiling, before pushing open the glass door, the small bell attached to the top of it giving wings to another one of Zuzu's angels.

Twenty minutes later I was back on the interstate. For the past three years I had been living in Charleston managing a high-end seafood restaurant. During the spring of my sophomore year in college I got a job at a sports bar. The restaurant business had been the only one I had known since. I traveled up and down the east coast for the first seven years, never staying at one place for more than six months. I got good at it. I went from sports bars, to local pubs, to corporate restaurants, ending up in fine dining. I bartended for a bit, but it didn't suit me. I hated being trapped. Not able to walk away. I put my notice in as soon as I arrived home.

CHAPTER TWO

Three days later I pulled into the parking lot of Stem. The building itself looked more like someone's home than a restaurant. Two stories of beige wood trimmed in white, came together after fifteen feet of flat roof on either side in a low-grade sloping peak, giving the appearance when standing directly in front of it, that it was the realization of an architect who had never fully given up his blocks. A deep porch supported with white rectangular columns ran the length of the front. No tables or chairs occupied the space, but on the far left-side, a hammock had been strung. In the center of the second story triangle was a large picture window filled with white curtains.

The restaurant, located on the north-eastern edge of Decatur, an urbanized suburb of Atlanta, was sandwiched between a progressive health studio on the left—its purple and white sign in the shape of a lotus blossom tethered between two transplanted stalks of green bamboo, offering classes in yoga, meditation, as well as nutrition—and a nail salon on the right. Across the slim, but busy two-lane street was a small used car dealership. I walked slowly through the Georgia humidity, pulled open the front door and stepped inside. A man with a salt and peppered crew cut was bent over the bar cutting limes. While my entrance had no effect on him, the soft click of the door closing behind me grabbed his attention. He glanced up with a look that said he didn't want to be bothered—but only for a split second. If I hadn't been watching closely I would have only seen the welcoming, practiced smile that spread quickly across his face. "Can I help you?" he said.

"I'm here to see Jim. Jim Steward. My name is George Muirhill."

"Yeah. Uh, just a sec. I'll let him know you're here," he said as he reluctantly left his limes and disappeared around the corner to the left of the bar.

I stood alone in the dining room. In many ways it was the same dining room I had been spending my nights in for years, ever since I had graduated from casual to fine dining. Stark-white linens covered the tables. The napkins were black and folded into neat squares. Sometimes they had been gray or dark brown. And instead of squares, they had been rectangles or triangles. Sometimes the water glasses were turned upside down. But the tablecloths had always been white. In the middle of these particular tablecloths, exactly at the intersection of the two creases that ran from the middle of one side of the table to the other, sat an opaque votive candle holder. A white wine stem rested above each knife.

"George," a baritone voice intoned, pulling my eyes to its unlikely source. The timbre sounded as though it should have belonged to an NFL lineman, but the man who strode towards me with his right hand extended was as thin as a reed and at best average height. "Jim Steward," he said as he gripped my hand.

"George Muirhill."

"Bruce said I'd regret it if I didn't meet with you. Said you were one of his best."

"I don't know about that," I said as my eyes drifted back to the tablecloths. I noticed that the one closest to me, a smaller table set for two, was slightly crooked. I had never taken compliments well.

"Are you looking for full time?"

"Yeah…uh…yes," I said as I refocused back on Jim.

"Bruce mentioned that you had managed before. Is that something you might be interested in doing again?"

"No," I responded sharply without thinking.

"Okay," he said, slightly taken aback.

"It's just that I like the hours. I like having my days to myself. I'm a musician." It wasn't exactly a lie. I had gone to school for music. The trumpet. But I hadn't played a note in years.

"I understand. Just curious," he responded. "So, I'd like to tell you a little about how we do things. I know you have experience in working in this caliber of restaurant, but every place has its subtleties."

"Please."

He walked over to a brown suede couch that sat to the right of the front door and motioned me to sit. He pulled a wooden chair from the closest corner of the room and positioned it directly across from me. A glass coffee table with a single book resting on its top was between us. On the cover was pictures of vintage baseball cards.

"We're a farm-to-table restaurant. Every day we have local farmers bring by fresh produce. All of our proteins—beef, chicken, fish, cured meat—come from sources where we are assured of their quality, purity, and humane treatment. The menu is dictated as much by what is in peak season as by what Chef wants to cook. We take pride in the food we serve. Pride in the fact we are not only offering delicious dishes, but sustainable ones as well. We recycle. We compost. Chef has a small garden behind the restaurant where we grow fresh herbs. Food, obviously, is a huge part of what we do and who we are. But it isn't the whole picture. Service is just as important. The balance—the marriage of the two—is what we feel provides the best possible experience. Servers are respected here."

"That's different."

"Yes. We pride ourselves on our humility. Not to say that we aren't very confident in what we do. But we don't let ego get in the way of what we are trying to accomplish. Our name, "Stem" comes from that. Our goal of an eloquent but not pretentious dining experience, stems from our commitment not to stray from the ideals we created this restaurant from. Another reason for the name is our emphasis on wine. In particular pairing wine with food. How is your wine knowledge?"

"Pretty good. I helped Bruce with the list last year, but I'm not certified or anything."

"Education—constantly trying to improve ourselves—is a big part of our culture. Every day at line-up Chef goes over every dish—each ingredient if it's the first day on the menu—and then any allergy concerns. I'll be honest," he said with a deep chuckle, "I think about half the time it's just because someone doesn't like the taste of something. But we deal with it regardless. We also go over all of the wine pairings for the menu as well as for the tasting menu every day. All the information that you need to succeed as a server will be given to you."

As impressed as I was with how Jim was describing the restaurant, my mind drifted. And while I continued to look right at him, my focus blurred. All of a sudden, a clap of abrupt quiet brought me back. Jim had stopped speaking and was looking at me as though he was waiting for a response. I can usually zone out like that and still pick up enough to seem engaged and follow the major points of a conversation, but I must have missed what he said. I took a risk, understanding the direction of the interview so far and confident that I could walk it back if need be.

"Yes."

"Good. How about Tuesday at three?"

Realizing he had inquired about me coming in to train or observe, I quickly reengaged.

"What should I wear?"

"What you have on is fine. Just lose the tie. We give the option of black, white, or gray dress shirts. You're choice."

"Okay. Thanks," I said as I stood up with him and gripped his outstretched hand. "I'll be here."

"I look forward to it," he said with a smile and a slight nod of his head before turning back towards the dining room.

I looked over to the bar and the bartender was gone. A solitary lime, still whole, its only inhabitant.

CHAPTER THREE

When I arrived back at the restaurant, Jim was standing at the bar looking at an invoice. He noticed me and placed the piece of paper back on the varnished wood.

"George, great to see you," he said reaching out to shake my hand.

"Yes, sir. Thank you."

He turned his head towards the dining room and half-shouted at one of the servers polishing a water glass. "Trey. Hey, Trey. C'mere." A stocky man with a jet-black full but neatly trimmed beard put down the glass and began to walk towards us. "Trey, this is George," Jim said as he approached.

"Trey. Nice to meet you," he said, extending his right arm. His grip was like a vice.

"George. You as well," I replied squeezing his hand as hard as I could.

"Trey, George is going to be with us for service tonight. I'd like him to follow you."

"Sounds good." he said with a nod before turning back towards the dining room. I followed. "We all have assigned side-work depending on what section we are in," he said once we returned to the water glass he was polishing before, "but I like to go ahead and polish my section. I'll give you a quick run down of the table numbers." Side-work was a part of every restaurant. I'm not exactly sure how the term permeated the entire culture at every level, but the daily tasks that had to be accomplished to prepare the restaurant for service and then break it back down again, as well as "running" side-work, which were the tasks accomplished as the night moved forward, were as much a staple of the business as the food. And at least in my experience there was always one server that probably should have been let go multiple times but for the ferocity with which they accomplished their side-work before, during, and after the shift. Like keeping around a baseball player that couldn't really hit or field, but could lay down a perfect bunt. Most days you wondered why they were there in the first place. But occasionally they were the reason why you won.

"Okay, sure," I said, pulling a pen and a small spiral bound note pad out of my pocket.

"So starting with that deuce (table of two) closest to the bar—that's ten. All of the tables towards the back of the restaurant are the teens: ten, eleven, twelve, thirteen, fourteen, and fifteen. The row behind it with the circular tables as well as squares—those are usually four-tops—are the twenties: twenty through twenty-six. This row that we're on is the thirties."

"Thirty through thirty-five?"

"Yes."

"Got it."

"The booths are the forties. Starting with forty and then moving back to forty-five."

"Okay," I said as I jotted all of this down.

"That table up those couple of steps at the back of the restaurant—that's sixty. It usually sits four to six, but we have a larger table top out back that can get it up to ten or twelve. How long have you been in the business?" he said, changing the subject.

"About twenty years."

"Twenty-five myself. Where were you last?"

"Charleston."

"Oh. That's cool. This is a good gig. Almost everyone here is a pro, so they don't mess with us very much. As long as we stay on point."

"Nice."

"The most important thing to remember here—if you get the job—is not to try and be a hero. We get busy. And Jim doesn't overstaff. The money can be really good, but there's going to be times when you need to ask for help. Do it. Ask Jim if you need to. He won't think any less of you. I promise. He'll respect you for it."

"Heard," I said, as I finished polishing the last glass on the table.

"Section looks good," he said turning towards a dark brown curtain that was across the small aisle at the edge of the dining room. He held it open and motioned me inside. Behind the curtain was the server station. A coffee grinder, tea urn, and hot water tower sat on the stainless-steel counter. A multitude of different sized containers used for cream, sugar cubes, simple syrup, packets of sweetener, olive oil, or anything else that a guest might need sat above them on a shelf of the same material. Built into the counter on the right side was an ice well and a small sink. A woman in her early thirties was cutting lemons to the right of the ice well as Trey and I walked in.

"Hey Maria."

"'Sup Trey," she said without turning around.

"This is George."

"Oh. Hi," she said, turning around and reaching out her right hand. "Maria."

"George. Nice to meet you," I said as I shook her hand. She was pretty. She had red hair that fell to her shoulders and bright blue eyes. Her ears were each pierced three times and a small birthmark towards the bottom of her neck, right above her left collar bone, was shaped like a crescent moon. She smiled as she let go of my hand.

"Follow me," Trey said as he continued to walk through the server station and into the kitchen. Early nineties grunge was playing on a portable speaker bouncing off of all of the metal in the room. I followed Trey past the dish pit and towards the line. The line was where all of the food was executed. Now it was being used for prep. As we turned a corner to go back into the server station, I saw a young man cleaning a whole fish. "See the loop we just made?" Trey said, grabbing a stack of trays from a wooden shelf built into the wall to the left of where we reentered the server station.

"Yeah," I said, looking at Maria. I quickly refocused back to Trey.

"The one we went out of. That's the only way you go. The one we came in through from the kitchen. That's the only way you go. Got it?"

"Got it."

"Otherwise accidents happen."

"Makes sense." I said back.

"Okay. Follow me." We walked back out through the curtain and into the dining room. "There's one more table that you haven't seen," he said as he turned right and walked towards the back of the restaurant. To the right of the raised floor where table sixty sat, separated from that table by a raised wooden wall, was another brown curtain. Trey pushed it to the side. "This is our only private dining space. It's called the Wine Room even though the actual wine room is on the other side of the kitchen. A large wooden table big enough for at least ten chairs sat in a dark room. Votives sat in built-in cubbies along all four walls. A small chandelier hung above the table.

"What's up asshole!" A voice from behind us said. Another server walked into the room. He flipped a switch to the right of the curtain and the chandelier lit up. I guessed he was around thirty. He had a goofy smile on his face and his blond hair had way too much gel in it. "Thomas." he said, nodding at me, seeing that I was in the room as well.

"George."

"Good to meet ya," he said back as he turned his attention to the table. "Well, I've got a table in here tonight, boys. The Fulsons. Need to get this ready."

Trey didn't say anything back, only walked into the dining room. "Remember when I said that almost everyone here was a pro?" he said quietly as we walked over to where he had set the stack of trays down when we left the server station.

"Yeah."

"That's the exception."

I chuckled.

"He's the assistant somm. Jim is the one who actually writes the list and does the pairings. I really don't think he does more than inventory. But ever since he got his level two pin, if there's a table that is going to want to geek out on wine, it's his." He stepped quickly into the server station and then came directly back out holding a bottle of Windex and two linens. He tossed one to me and then walked over to the small ledge that sat to the left of the brown curtain and picked up a tray and sprayed it with blue liquid before handing over the bottle.

Thirty minutes later we gathered in the private dining room for lineup, a run-down of the night's reservations, any changes on food or wine, or anything else service related that Jim needed to go over. Besides myself there were five other servers sitting around the long wooden table as well as the same bartender who had been cutting limes. Each of us had been given a white paper copy of the `a la carte menu, with the courses from the blind tasting menu on the back. Besides Trey, Thomas, and Maria, two other people sat at the long wooden table. The bigger of the two, Mark, introduced himself to me earlier in a thick southern twang; the other server, sitting to Mark's left was Merlin. "Like the wizard," Trey told me just before we walked into the room at the back of the restaurant.

I looked at each of the faces of the other servers in the room. They were the same faces I had seen my entire time working in restaurants. Sure, physically they were different, but there's something about the transparency among the relationships you develop while working in a dining room that cause the people around you to appear slightly blurred. In any work environment superficial relationships are a necessity. Mostly, work is discussed—usually complained about. A "work friend" feels like someone you have an actual connection with, even though you know that in the back of your head, as soon as either of you left, you'd probably never speak again. In the restaurant business it's a little different. Everyone in the front of the house interacts confidently with strangers for a living. We are amorphous—changing our personality to fit the encounter. Our practiced graciousness having given over completely to instinct. So when it comes to the interactions between each other, while we all play along that they are genuine, we can never really be sure. Over the years, the names have changed, but the faces are always the same.

"Okay. Good evening everyone," Jim said, sitting at the head of the table in his deep baritone. "If you haven't met him already, this is George," he said, motioning to me with his right hand. "He's going to be with us tonight to see if this might be a good fit for him," he paused briefly, "or if he is a good fit for us". As far as the night goes, we have forty-five on the books. There's two larger parties, so tonight let's pool." Thomas cleared his throat and rolled his eyes. He had expected to have that private party all to himself. If Jim hadn't decided to pool all of the tips everyone brought in and divide them equally, Thomas probably would have made more than anyone else. "The menu is the same, but I've changed one of the pairings on the tasting menu. The trout is switching from Riesling to Gewürztraminer. Also, even though it's still on the menu, we are out of half bottles of blanc de blanc." He paused again, this time longer than before. "I have two service notes for today. The first is that we all know it's a little on the slow side tonight, and on slow nights is when mistakes happen. Focus. Please. The other note is that because it is slower and you shouldn't be running around too much, use this as an opportunity to be perfect. Remember, it's all in the details."

As Jim was going over the last service note, a thin man with white scraggly hair nearly the same shade as the starched chef's coat he wore, ducked quietly into the room. "Hello, Chef," Jim said, stepping back from the head of the table and allowing the older man to take his place. He looked around the room, slowly making eye contact with everyone. "The menu is the same as it was yesterday," he said in a calm voice. "But let's go ahead and go over any allergies for anyone who wasn't here. Are there any special restrictions or requests, Jim?" he asked, turning his head towards the doorway.

"No, Chef. Nothing out of the ordinary. Two gluten free diners as well as one shellfish allergy."

Trey pulled out a pen and motioned for me to do the same and pulled the menu, `a la carte side up, in front of him on the table. "'G' is gluten, 'D' is dairy, and 'S' is shellfish," he said under his breath. "Circle it if it can be omitted." I met his gaze and nodded.

Chef proceeded to go quickly through the entire menu. He mentioned when a dish had any of the major allergy concerns and then told us whether that component could be left off. Twice he said that a gluten component could be left off if necessary, but he wouldn't recommend it, pausing each time after he said this and making eye contact with everyone in the room, his head slightly cocked and the expression on his face saying that if absolutely necessary he would do it, but he didn't want to because the food would suffer. I watched Trey write down the letters he had gone over with me on the outside margin next to each of the dishes Chef spoke about. As soon as Chef finished, he wished us a good service and then slipped quietly out of the room. Jim then went over the wine pairings for the tasting menu that evening, before thanking us for being there as we all stood up.

The night went well. I followed Trey for the majority of service. Once he realized that I knew what I was doing, he let me jump in and help him clear and then mark with silverware the separate courses of last two tables that he had been given. Compared to when we were setting up, he barely said a word. Most of his direction was non-verbal, usually just making eye contact with me and then looking at what needed to be done next. He was warm with his tables, but didn't spend any time at all talking about anything that wasn't directly related to dinner. The night started at forty-five people, but there was a good amount of walk-ins, finishing at fifty-eight. At close to a hundred dollars a head, that was solid. Only one of Trey's tables wanted the blind tasting menu, and they got it with the wine pairings. The other four ordered off of the `a la carte menu. As the last few tables finished up in the dining room, Jim found me and asked me to join him at the bar.

"How did your night go?"

"Good. Trey is a pro."

"Yeah. He's one of our best. He had good things to say about you as well."

"Thanks." As I said this, Maria placed a plate in front of me at the bar. The bartender, Jack, placed a fork and knife on either side of the dish.

"Can I pour you a pairing?" Jim said.

"Yeah. That would be great. Thanks," he nodded to Jack who handed him a bottle across the bar with one hand as he placed a wine glass down in front of me with the other. He was efficient—remarkably smooth.

"Gewürz," Jim said as he poured almost a full glass. "To go with the trout. On the plate is a parsnip puree, with roasted sunchokes and a dill-carrot sauce."

"Thanks again," I said as I put together a bite with all of the components on the plate on my fork. As I began to lift the utensil off of the plate, Jim spoke again.

"Do you know why we chose to pair this dish with Gewürztraminer, George?"

I rested my fork back on the plate and looked at the dish. "The carrots?"

"Very good." he said, standing up and then walking back into the dining room.

While I wasn't a sommelier like Jim, I definitely undersold myself at the interview. From my experience most managers like more of a project—someone they can mold—rather than someone who could do their job. I had managed beverage programs at a few restaurants in the past. I knew how to pair food and wine. In fact I liked it. Much more so than learning about the specific climate of a region or how a particular type of rocky soil causes the vine to struggle, producing better grapes. That was all well-and-good, but a good pairing was a beautiful thing. I think I kind of had a knack for it too. Jim did as well. The dish itself was fantastic. The trout was cooked perfectly—the skin crispy and delicate—and the rest of the components all complimented each other. But with the wine it sang.

As I finished the dish, Jim returned to the seat next to mine. "What did you think?"

"It was delicious. Thanks again." I wanted to go into all of the intricacies that had been spinning in my mind, but I didn't. I didn't want to overdo it.

"Well George, I'd like to offer you a position here if you'd like to join our team."

"Yes. Thank you. I really appreciate it," I said as I reached out to shake his hand.

"Good. Can you come in on Thursday to start training?"

"Yes. I'll be here."

"Three thirty, please. I'll need you to fill out some paperwork."

"Sure thing."

"I look forward to it," he said before turning back to the dining room.

For as big as he was, Trey moved like a cat. As I stood up from my chair, he stepped around me to grab the dirty plate and wine glass from the bar. I almost jumped. Almost. "Good news?" he said with raised eyebrows and the hint of a grin.

"Yeah."

"Good. I'll see you soon then." He walked away just as silently as he had come.

I had two days before I started training. As I drove back to the motel I thought about Liberty. Now that I was here how was I possibly going to find her? The city was huge. But the same feeling that brought me to her mother's doorstep still lingered in my bones.

CHAPTER FOUR

I hate getting my hair cut. Having to sit there for twenty minutes looking into that giant mirror while the person cutting my hair keeps trying to make small talk, is torture. I've never liked the way I looked. Even though my appearance improves while I sit and stare at myself, I can't help but to only notice the bags under my eyes and the almost double chin that seems to grow in real time. It's a necessary evil though—having to sit in that chair and see all of my flaws. I avoid it as long as I can—let my hair get just long enough that it doesn't start to grow over my ears—before having to do it again.

After suffering through a haircut at a place a few blocks from the motel I had been staying at, I began to drive around looking for a more permanent place to live. As haircuts go, it was better than most. The woman who cut my hair was Asian—Vietnamese I think. After inviting me to sit down in her chair and then asking how I wanted my hair cut, she didn't say another word until she held a small, square mirror behind my head and asked my approval of my hairline. No small talk. Beautiful.

I drove around for about two hours looking for a place. The ones that I liked the most were too expensive—there's no way I'm spending over a thousand a month for a one bedroom. The ones that were affordable were pretty run down. Possibilities, if I couldn't find anything better. Frustrated with the whole process, I decided to get something to eat. I ended up at a pizza place across the street from Emory University. I sat at the bar and ordered a small white pizza. It was good, but could have used more ricotta. The place was pretty busy for three o'clock in the afternoon. Only two of the red leather booths that looked like they had been ripped out of vintage Caddies that hugged the walls were empty. A few square wooden tables filled out the middle of the dining room, and those were vacant as well. The bartender was around my age, maybe a few years younger. I asked her for a few recommendations on bars either in the area or in Atlanta as a whole. She rattled off a few and then grabbed some printer paper from the register and wrote them down for me. I thanked her and settled up.

"See you soon!" she said enthusiastically behind me as I opened the front door and she noticed the fifty percent tip I had left.

"Thanks," I said as I walked out. I didn't ask her to write the names of those bars down. She had done that on her own. Great service. A touch that wasn't necessary or expected. I respect that. The pizza place was in a strip of other restaurants, coffee shops, and retail spots. To the right of the strip was a residential street that led into a neighborhood. I decided to forget about finding a place for a little while and do some exploring. Interestingly enough, I was able to do both.

After winding around twisty and hilly tree-lined side streets for fifteen minutes, I found myself looking at much bigger houses than I had seen so far in the neighborhood. Then to my right a golf course replaced the houses that had edged that side of the street and the houses across from it on the other side grew even larger. I noticed a "For Rent" sign on one of the front lawns, staked close to a large, brick mailbox. When a house of that size is rented, a sign isn't put in the front yard. A service is used. I parked in front of the house and wrote down the phone number written neatly in black marker on the bottom of the sign. The house was brick—the same as the mailbox. It was three stories high and a large, manicured green lawn stretched across the width of it like a moat. On the far-left side was the driveway. At the end of the long, black length of pavement was what looked like a carriage house.

I called the number as I drove away and it was answered after a few rings by a woman. She was very polite, but to the point. The carriage house was for rent, but she and her husband hadn't listed it online. They were waiting for the right kind of person to inquire. They were both lawyers. Successful ones it would seem. They were looking for someone quiet and responsible to rent the carriage house and then look after their three dogs when they are out of town. "We've been having a service come by and look after them the last few times we have traveled, but I just get the feeling that they're only coming by and feeding them, not spending some time with them as I asked. My husband and I will be home tonight around six if you'd like to come by and have a look."

"Yes ma'am. That would be great."

After taking a shower and putting on a freshly ironed shirt, I drove back over to the house and pulled into the driveway at five fifty-five. Immediately the front door opened and a short and stocky woman with vivid red hair and a business suit walked out. "George?" she called out to me as I got out of my car.

"Yes, ma'am," I called back.

She quickly stepped down the five stairs that led to a sidewalk that connected to the driveway at the edge of the house.

"Nice to meet you, George," she said flatly. "Winifred Stroud. My husband Gerald isn't home yet, but I can show you around."

"Yes ma'am. Nice to meet you."

"Come on then. Right this way," she said, turning away from me and towards the carriage house, her heeled shoes clacking briskly on the pavement—pit pat, pit pat, pit pat. "Come on." she said without looking back.

"Yes, ma'am," I said picking up my pace. I caught up to her as she neared the carriage house. But she took an abrupt right and began to walk towards the black wired metal fence that enclosed the backyard. As she reached the gate on the far right side of the fence closest to the house, three massive black dogs with patches of brown on their coats came barreling towards her.

"There's my babies!" she said, her pointed business-like tone from before now turning mushy, like that of a grandmother greeting a five-year old grandchild before pinching their cheek. "Come on George. Come over here and meet my darlings." I hesitated. Those "darlings" were scary as hell. "Come on, now." As I began to walk towards her she lifted the latch on the gate. I stopped in my tracks. "There's nothing to worry about," she said as she motioned me over to her with her other hand. I stood behind her as she pushed the gate open. "Sit!" she snapped at the three rambunctious dogs. To my surprise, they did just that. I followed her into the backyard, closing the gate and letting down the latch behind me. The three dogs sat in a wobbly line in front of us looking eagerly at her. She pointed to the biggest of the three on the far right. "That's Harold. And that's Maude," she said as she pointed to the smallest of the three on the far left. "And this, their son, is Licorice." Licorice was just as tall as Harold, but leaner, not nearly as muscular. His tongue fell out of his jaw sideways as he panted with anticipation. "They're harmless, George." she said as she walked towards Harold and rubbed him affectionately on his head. I hesitated a moment and then took a step forward towards the dogs. Licorice bounded to his feet and then launched himself at me. I fell beneath the weight of him terrified. Then I heard laughter. And realized that I wasn't being mauled to death; rather my face was being licked like an ice cream cone. "Back!" she shouted after she stopped laughing. "Licorice, back!" After the second command he climbed off of me and went over to her. I stood up and brushed myself off. I could still feel the dog's saliva coating my face. I ran my hands over my cheeks, but that only seemed to make things worse. I looked over to her. She was fighting back a grin. "Sit," she said sternly to the young dog. He walked back over to where he had been before and sat down, his tongue falling out of his mouth as his hindquarters hit the ground.

"Harmless?" I said to her.

"Yes, dear. Harmless. Licorice is still learning. He just likes you. I supposed you'd like to see the carriage house?" she said as she began to walk back the few paces towards the gate.

"Yes, ma'am."

"Let's go then."

I followed, but kept the three dogs in the corner of my eye until I was safely on the other side of the metal fence.

The inside of the carriage house was smaller than it looked from the outside. The walls were covered in wallpaper that must have been from the seventies—burnt yellow with deep green fronds curving to the left and right. But it was spotless. I couldn't see a speck of dust or a lone fingerprint on any of the windows. It had the feeling of not being lived in for a long time. "We don't use the garage," she said, still standing in the doorway, having let me in first. "It's just for storage."

"Yes, ma'am," I said over my shoulder as I walked into the kitchen. The stove was small, but at the four burners were gas, not electric.

"The bedroom is over here," she said from the entrance to the kitchen, and then turned and began to walk in the other direction once she saw my head swivel towards the sound of her voice. I followed. To my surprise a large bed filled the majority of the cramped room. "You can use this if you want. It was here when we bought the place."

"Thanks. That would be great." It must have been a king-sized mattress and box spring, but that wasn't what was so impressive about the thing. The frame was one of those over-sized ones where the bed posts continued upward and then were connected by rods at the top of them that were supposed to hold curtains. But there weren't any.

"So what do you think, George? You seem like a responsible adult." the squat woman said, this time standing in front of me. "If you want it, it'll be seven hundred a month, utilities included. There's a cable hook-up as well. You'd need to get your own box. You don't have an issue looking after my darlings do you?"

"No, ma'am." I lied a little. I was intimidated by those beasts behind the metal gate. But everything else was perfect. "Thank you. This is great."

"Good," she said as she walked out of the bedroom and towards the door and the wooden set of stairs that led down to the garage floor. "Just call me or text to let me know when you'd like to move in. I'll get you the key. You should meet my husband soon. He'll be very happy that we have found a tenant."

CHAPTER FIVE

I'm terrified by routine. Somewhere in my late twenties I began to notice other people's: the way that they make a cup of coffee, or cut their sandwich. Or hearing them talk about the only route that they take to work. And they talk about it like it theirs. Like they somehow own this series of turns that leads them from one place to another. They refer to their routines as "My way to work," or, "You know I have to have my coffee just the way I like it." It's kind of ridiculous if you think about it. Sure, you've found a good route to work, or you know you like steamed milk in your coffee. But these routines seem to take a hold of folks. They embrace them and seldom stray. It seems like most people are so determined to define, label, and feel in control of their worlds that they miss out on so much actual life. What terrifies me most is how routines affect time. You take the same way to work, drink the same cup of coffee, have pizza every Friday, trim your fingernails on Sunday, and then like that, ten years have gone by.

For a while I embraced chaos completely, hoping to slow down time as much as possible. But no routine is the same thing. You have to have enough structure to mark the time, or it speeds up just as if you were lost in your own constructs of control. So I have a few routines that I regard in the same way I would a wild animal. I keep them in front of me and make sure not to let them slip out of my field of vision. But for most of my day to day I make an effort to do things more randomly. I make sure to go different ways to get places, try new things even if I'm not sure I'll like them. I keep enough structure in my life so as not to get swept away by the chaos, but I let myself feel it everyday.

Chaos, I think, is what drew me to the restaurant business. Because really that's what it is. Controlled chaos. At least the perception of control. It is a business that spends all day making plans—prepping food, booking tables, figuring out where each reservation will be seated—all until every detail is covered. Then the doors open and it all of that planning goes to shit. Sure, you hear of rare days where all of the reservations show up on time, leave on time, and their food comes out perfectly. But that always happened to someone else. Some anecdote told through the thick head of a freshly poured beer. Most nights, the plan becomes moot by the middle of service, if not sooner. Then you have to improvise. And that's what we do. And at the fine dining level, we have to do it in a way that makes the people sitting in front of white table cloths feel as though the plan worked to perfection the entire time.

Ultimately, it's the same game regardless of where you are. Read your table, make them feel as though the experience is being dictated by them, even though you are the one subtly pushing and pulling the night to meet your responsibilities, while moving around the restaurant as efficiently as possible. But every place has its own character. Having spent the last decade in fine dining I found it amazing how many different ways have been devised to give "proper service." At some places I, along with my fellow servers, had to bring an entire table's food to the table at the exact same time, stand behind each guest—be it two or ten—and then in perfect unison place the dish in front of the diner with our left hand—always ladies first—before placing the dish in our right hand in complete unison to the remaining seats. In that restaurant, if you could do it gracefully enough, you could have a table of four, or even five and clear that table of plates by yourself. In another place that I worked, however, food was brought to the table usually piecemeal, rarely dropped in unison, but if you had a table larger than three people, you had to stop what you were doing to go and find another server, server assistant, or even a manager to clear a table gracefully as a team. Server assistants could make your night smooth or a living hell depending on whether or not they liked you. I always made sure to put a few extra dollars in their pockets on busy nights. Seemed to help me stay on the good side. It wasn't the money, though. It was the respect.

As far as overall service goes I guess every GM has their preferences. You'd think there would be one decided upon way to do things. But the uniqueness of every restaurant, from the style of cuisine, to the physical layout of the building, always dictated that something had to bend to get through the night. Plus, if every single guideline of proper service that has been thought up was followed, serving dinner would be impossible.

On my first night training Trey told me that the particular emphasis at Stem—of Jim in particular—was table maintenance. "Look," he said as we walked toward the front of the dining room after a brief line up, "your tables have to be on point. If you're getting hammered make sure your tables are tight. Jim would rather you ask him to open a bottle of wine so that you can crumb a table instead of that table not being immaculate while you popped a cork. Trust me, George, I learned the hard way. Where I came from, crumbing a table or pulling an empty glass was important, but not like it is here. He's got a thing for lines. It's not a cleanliness thing. He's not a germaphobe or OCD about how a table should look. You'll hear him talk about 'clean lines', trust me. It's a little much, but it's not my call. Basically, what he says is that the negative space of a table is what allows the lines of the table and the dining room to be elegant. Like a few crumbs or an empty rocks glass causes the tables or the silver to look crooked. Like I said, I don't see it, but I make sure that it gets done."

"Heard. Thanks, man,"

I followed Trey for the rest of the night watching how he interacted with his tables and how he moved around the dining room. Well, more so where things were kept around the dining room. Most of the silverware was in the server station, but a tall thin mahogany cabinet had been placed to the outside of the private room as well, which contained two shelves of glassware, two trays of silver, and three marking trays. Marking trays were another staple of fine dining. As efficient as it would be to grab a handful of silverware to go and replace on your table between courses, that was not allowed. A marking tray, which could be anything from a metal rectangle or circle with slip-resistant lining, to a simple plate lined with a precisely folded linen, was necessary when bringing silverware to a table. Trays were also needed for any drink or piece of glassware that went to a table as well. If you had already placed down your stems and wine trivet—the small silver coaster that just fit the bottom of a wine bottle—you didn't need a tray for the bottle of wine. That was the only exception as long as it was carried through the dining room gracefully, and with the label facing out.

The night was somewhat busy, but manageable. I was able to help Trey clear some tables as well as run some food. I didn't interact much with the guests, but I knew that would come. At the end of the night, I stayed until Trey was finished and helped him do his side work—polishing the crystal glassware that had been used that night. With two of us it didn't take that long. Afterwards Trey showed me how to do his checkout and then we brought it to Jim in his office.

"So, how did your night go?" Jim asked me after Trey walked back down the narrow staircase that stretched from the cramped second floor to right behind a flimsy door that opened up into the hallway that led from the bar to the kitchen.

"Good. Thanks."

"That's good to hear." He paused for a moment and looked off to the side before refocusing back on me. "So, George, how many more training shifts do you think you'll need before you'll be ready for a small section on the floor?"

The question caught me off guard. I stared back for a long moment before answering. "Uh... I don't know. I guess two or three. I've got to get down the computer. I feel pretty good about the menu. But it changes, right?"

"The menu does change," Jim said, smiling. "So today is Thursday. Do you think that if you trained with Trey again the next two shifts you could take a few tables on Tuesday?"

I was still quite confused. "Yeah, I think so."

"That's great, George," he said as he turned his attention away from me and sat down at the desk. The desk was by far the most composed aspect of the room. Wine bottles from countless nights—good ones worth keeping—were balanced on almost every surface in the compact office. Maps of wine regions—Bordeaux, Burgundy, Napa, Sonoma—that must have been from the seventies hung haphazardly from the walls with brass tacks. In between the colorful maps were signed menus from wine dinners or private events. More than one used wine glass sat on the squat table in the corner stacked with books or the leaning filing cabinet to the right of the door. The chaos of the room was like service itself. But Jim's desk was the calm in the storm: neat, orderly, and efficient. "I'll see you tomorrow, then," I said just before I turned towards the stairs. He looked up at me once more with a smile.

"Thank you, George. Would you please close the door behind you?"

I nodded.

CHAPTER SIX

I showed up to the restaurant for my final training shift on Saturday. I had spent the previous night with Trey doing almost all of the computer work and fronting the last three tables that we were assigned for the night myself. I felt better about the workings of the place, but was relieved to have another night of working with Trey before I was on my own. Unfortunately that wasn't the case. Two steps into the building Jim popped up from behind the bar. "George," he said as he rounded the edge of the dark counter and walked quickly towards me. "How are you doing today?"

"I'm good. Thanks."

He motioned for me to follow him into the small alcove to the left of the door where a small maroon couch and two cushioned chairs of the same color were positioned in a semi-circle. He didn't sit down. "Do you think you could maybe take a two-table section on your own tonight, George?"

"Yeah...uh, sure."

"What do you think about three?" he said after a moment's pause with the look of a five-year old asking for a second helping of dessert spreading across his face.

"I think I could do that." I responded after a measured breath.

"That's great, George! Thank you so much. If you could give me just a minute I'll add you to the floor chart."

"No problem." He walked briskly towards the host stand.

I was assigned three deuces in a compact section right next to Trey. I was nervous when I approached my first table, worried that I would be asked a question that I didn't have the answer to. But I realized quickly that the young couple that sat in front of me was wrapped up in each other to the point that I wouldn't have to worry. My shoulders relaxed and I fell into old routines. I paid more attention to him so he wouldn't think I was flirting with his lady, but every time I asked a question, he looked to her as soon as he answered, hoping for approval. This was an easy one: make him look good in front of her while making sure she got what she wanted. Piece of cake.

My second table was easy as well. Another couple, but older— much older. From the generation where you ordered your martini as soon as the waiter arrived and didn't discuss anything, especially food, until both glasses were empty. They sipped on their gin martinis, both very dry, for almost twenty minutes. This worked out perfectly because my third table of the night sat down ten minutes later and I needed the time. They were a handful.

A father and his daughter. She must have been about eighteen. She was short. Like really short. Less than five feet. And while she wasn't fat, she wasn't skinny either. There was a stoutness to her. Her square jaw and short brown hair that hung in a straight line just below her chin reminded me of a staunch German actress from some

World War II movie. Had at any time she stared at me with ire and yelled, "schnell!" I would have taken it in stride. Dad was pretty much apathetic about the whole of it. This didn't feel like his kind of place. His jacket, which he took off as soon as he saw other men not wearing one, was too small. Like it was from a previous life. Overall, he was completely average. He just wanted a beer in his hand and some food in front of him. But his daughter, the newly reformed vegan, she told me almost immediately, wanted not only me, but the entire restaurant to stand on its head for her. Her father never interjected, but I caught him rolling his eyes more than once. The first time, after he promptly ordered a beer and then sat and watched his daughter and I have a five-minute discussion about hot tea. She initially brought up the topic and asked what brand of tea we carried as well as the different types. I was about to excuse myself and go and grab the dessert menu which had all of the tea offerings on the back when I felt a tap on my back. Trey slid a menu into my right hand as I turned slightly towards him. I handed the menu to the young woman and then began to turn away and place the order for her dad's beer. "I'll give you a moment to look over the selections and I will be right back with the gentleman's beer," I said as I pivoted on my left heel.

"Thank you," he said.

"Wait," she said immediately. I slowly turned back around. "Is your tea loose leaf or bagged?"

I froze for about five seconds trying to recall what type of tea I had seen in the server station. Then it came to me—the metal tins with the type of tea labeled in white across the front. "Loose leaf, ma'am."

"Good," she said, still looking at the back of the dessert menu. "I don't see a mint tea. Do you not have a mint tea?"

I bent over and as politely as I could muster gestured with an open hand exactly where she was looking. "I'm sorry ma'am, but these are the only teas that we have to offer. If you're looking for an herbal tea, we have a very nice Chamomile."

"I don't understand why you wouldn't have mint," she said turning her stare from the page to me. I glanced at her father who again rolled his eyes.

"I'm very sorry. Would you care for a few more moments to look over the menu before you decide?"

"Well, since you don't have mint tea, what I would like is a cup of hot water with fresh mint to steep in it. I'll make my own," she said very self-assuredly. "And I'd like honey too.

"Very good, ma'am. I will get the hot water and fresh mint together as well as the gentleman's beer," I said more to him than to her. Even though honey wasn't vegan. He looked like he needed that drink as fast as possible. I began to turn away again.

"Excuse me," she piped up just as quick as the last time I tried to leave. "Can you please go over the vegan options?" Her father wiped his dry brow and exhaled forcefully.

"Let me speak with Chef and then I will be able to go over everything that we can offer you today." Her mouth began to open again, so I quickly cut her off. "There might be something off of the menu that we could prepare for you. I want you to have all of the options we can offer." As the last few words fell out of my mouth, I had already begun to turn and then pushed off of my right foot quickly and walked away from their table as fast as decorum would allow.

After placing the order for the dad's beer in the computer, I went to the bar to ask for a few sprigs of mint. My initial inquiry was met back with a suspicious stare from Jack. My explanation flew out of my mouth in a clump. It must have sounded like gibberish. But thankfully he seemed to understand, rolled his eyes at the whole of it and handed me what I needed. I rushed into the server station and immediately filled a teapot with hot water and shoved the mint inside to steep. I had to get back in my section to check on my other two tables. When I approached the needy chick and her dad, my first table, the young couple, was finishing up their entrees; the older couple had been nursing their martinis and had yet to order. That's what concerned me. Something in their posture gave me the impression that they wanted nothing to do with their server until they did, at which point they expected me to be standing there waiting. What I didn't need was the both of them looking around tying to find me. Once a table thought you were not on top of things, it didn't matter what you did from then on. Most start looking for other things to find issue with, even at the expense of their own enjoyment.

I set a small digital timer and placed it next to the steeping pot. As I began to rush out of the server station, Trey walked in. "Dessert menus are down on thirteen, and have the order for fourteen." My look in response was half terror and half relief. I didn't want to come across as though I couldn't handle three small tables. "You're good George," Trey said in return, in response to the look smeared over my face. "Trust me. Those kids are fine. And the older couple—the Johnstons—they're in here once a week. They don't give a damn who takes their order. They probably thought I was you."

"Oh. Okay. Thanks, man. I really appreciate it." I said back as relief edged out over the panic."

"No sweat, bro. I could see what you were dealing with at fifteen. Ouch. You better get back out there. Here's the order." he said, handing me a piece of paper. Can you read that?"

I looked at it quickly. "Yeah. Got it. Thanks again." He didn't respond, only slapped me on the shoulder and walked past me into the kitchen.

The rest of the night was smooth. Chef put together three courses for the vegan chick as well as a dessert. Her father clung to his beer like a life preserver, ordering another before the one currently in his hand was finished. He finished the last swallow of his fifth glass as he handed me his credit card before returning his attention to his phone. He held it up to me. "Beautiful, isn't it," he said with a smile. "All I've got to do is punch a few buttons and my own personal driver comes to pick me up." I saw the app on his phone saying that the car he'd ordered was three minutes away. "Makes things a whole lot bearable," he said with a wink. "You have a good night now."

"Yes, sir. You do the same—both of you." He didn't respond, just smiled as he motioned for his daughter to stand up. As they walked away I reached for the check on the table that he had just signed. I opened the manila colored folded piece of stiff paper with a small wine glass in black on the front of it. After dealing with that girl and then her father pretty much acknowledging how much of a pain in the ass she is, I was hoping for a good tip. I couldn't believe it when I saw the fifteen percent gratuity he had scribbled on the receipt. Really? Fifteen percent tells me that I did a bad job, not that I gave gracious service while dealing with a brat. Fifteen percent used to be an acceptable tip like thirty years ago. Today it means you had a problem, or you're cheap.

My night as a whole was okay. I waited on six tables in total and the older couple who barely acknowledged me for the entirety of their meal, and which was by far my easiest table, left me fifty dollars on a hundred and fifty-dollar check, which more than made up for the poor tip I received from the table which gave me the most work. Over all of my years in restaurants I haven't been able to come to a firm decision on whether I think a steady paycheck is actually better than the emotional ups and downs of living off of tips. There's something about the potential of making more money today than you did yesterday that is both comforting and scary. In a way, servers are like extremely conservative degenerate gamblers, always hoping and waiting for the big payday, but never leaving completely broke at the end of the night.

I was one of the first to finish with my tables, but unlike most restaurants, where finishing early meant going home before the other servers who still had tables, at Stem everyone stayed until close together and then did all of the side-work as a team. So I spent the last forty five minutes after my last table left, chatting with Trey and Maria. Trey mostly nodded. As the night wound down and silence slowly filled the building, all I could think of was Liberty.

CHAPTER SEVEN

I left Stem around twelve thirty—not that bad for a Friday night—with a hundred and forty dollars in my pocket. At the recommendation of the woman from the pizza place, I ended up in Virginia Highlands, an upper middle class neighborhood surrounded by a few patches of trendy bars and restaurants. I found myself around one at a place packed with ex frat boys and sorority girls, having given up their college letters for law offices and business suits.

I sat at the end of the bar closest to the door. It was loud. All of it. The noise itself as well as the people. I watched people coming and going while I sipped on a whiskey and ginger ale and thought about what she might be like now. I thought about the way I remembered her. Always in those green shoes, untied. Her dark brown hair constantly being tucked behind her ears so it didn't fall in her face when she was bent over her notebook writing. Her devious smile. Then thoughts shifted to a more recent time. When I made the decision to find her and drove home. Surrounded by all of the loudness I began to feel as alone as I did that day in my car.

I graduated high school in the Spring of 1998. I worked that summer at Pensdale's only hardware store, lugging bags of quick-dry cement and bales of pine straw in the oppressive Georgia heat. As miserable as it was, there was a peace to it—my exhaustion was a buffer helping to keep me numb. Helping me from not constantly thinking about what happened. Once the temperature began to drop it was time for me to begin my freshman year in college. I bought my first car with what I made over the summer—a 1984 Chevy Cavalier—off-white with only a radio to listen too. The last time that I saw exit fourteen—the winding two lane road that led to Pensdale—was in my rear-view mirror the day I left for school.

Seeing it again nearly twenty years later left me awash with nostalgia. Most people I've heard bring up nostalgia, do so with a sense of reverence—there's a warmth, like being wrapped in a childhood blanket. But for me it's always been cold. Stark. Making me feel that much more alone. Dark clouds filled the sky and the wind began to push and pull the tall Georgia pines that lined the sides of the road as I neared home. As I pulled into my parent's driveway, it began to rain. I got out of the car and walked through the falling drops of water—each like a subtle pin prick on my skin like when your leg falls asleep and goes numb—until I reached the front door. I put my hand on the knob, but then hesitated. I hadn't called to tell my parents I was coming home. So I rang the bell. A few seconds later my father answered the door.

"George! George!" he said enthusiastically as his stony blue eyes lit up and he grasped my hand. His grip from years as a general contractor was as strong as ever. "Come in. Come in." He ushered me into the living room. "May! May! George is here," he yelled in no particular direction. "George—"

"I hear you. I hear you," came my mother's voice from the kitchen. "You don't have to yell," she said as she came into the room. "George." Her face lit up with a smile. "I can't believe you're here." She closed the gap between the two of us quickly and by the time her arms were wrapped around me she was sobbing into my t-shirt. "I didn't think you'd ever come back," she said muffled into my chest.

"I know Mom."

I'd seen my parents at least once a year since I left, usually around the holidays. They would get into my father's old gray truck that still sat in the driveway and come to find me in whichever place I called home at the time. But there was something different about seeing them at home. They both looked older than I remembered. My father, even with his vice grip, seemed shorter. His hair now a lighter gray. He was beginning to look like an old man. My mother let go of me and took a few steps back towards my father. She wiped the tears from her eyes with one hand as she grasped my father's with her other. Last year, her hair had been dyed to the same auburn brown that I had always known, but it seemed faded now and her roots were coming in the same color as my father's. She looked up at him and then at me. Then she smiled. She had the most beautiful smile. It was so genuine. It began at her mouth and then radiated from her dark blue eyes. Seeing her smile caused me to do the same, for what felt like the first time in months. My smile was terrible. It looked like I had an itch that I just couldn't scratch and was trying to think about something else. So over the years I turned it more into a closed lipped smirk. But at this moment, standing in my childhood home, with my mother staring at me with shining eyes, I couldn't help but to fully let my emotion show through and smile as big as I had in years. Then the moment was gone. The weight of everything that brought me home crashing back onto my shoulders.

"Well, what would you like to drink, George?" my mother said, walking back towards the kitchen. "I'll get you something—and make a snack—and you can tell us about things. Would you like a soda?"

"No ma'am, just water," I said back like I was fifteen.

"Okay, hon'," she said from the next room. "I'll make something quick and then we can talk about how you've been. You know you haven't called in a few months."

"I know. I'm sorry," I called towards her.

"Don't worry about that, son," my father said to me, motioning for me to sit down on the brown leather sofa that was new to me. I remembered a dark green one, kind of a velvety material that pulled out into a very uncomfortable bed. "She just worries for no reason." I sat down on the brown leather and my father sat across from me in his chair—a wooden rocking chair that he built with his own hands when I was a kid. The cushion on it was different that before, but that chair looked as sturdy as ever. We both sat in silence until my mother returned from the kitchen.

She came back into the room carrying a tray in her left hand and my glass of ice water in her right. Her jeans swished as she walked with purpose towards the two of us. She wore a dark green blouse, almost the same color as the couch that was now gone. When she first came out of the kitchen when I first arrived, her hair had been in a loose bun; it now hung below her shoulders.

"Here we go," she said as she placed the white ceramic tray on the glass coffee table that sat between the sofa and my father. On one side of the tray was a pile of wheat crackers. On the other was small chunks of cheddar cheese and cherry tomatoes. After handing me the water, she sat down next to me on the couch. The three of us sat and ate crackers and cheese and popped cherry tomatoes as we talked for the next half an hour. Mostly small talk. She asked me if I'd been seeing anyone. He asked me about work. I told them that everything was the same as it always was. Charleston was great. The restaurant was staying busy. Bruce was still trying to get me to get back into managing on the nights when he wasn't there, and I still said no. I told my mom that I'd been on a few dates recently, which was a lie, but nothing serious. I could tell she wanted to ask me about Vanessa, but she didn't.

After the tray was empty, I told them that I needed to run out for a few minutes. My mother protested saying that I had just gotten home, so I promised I would be back for dinner as I stood up and walked towards the door. That seemed to satisfy her enough that I didn't feel too guilty as I got back into my car.

The memory faded as the lights of the bar were turned up and "last call" was announced. The bartender, a heavy-set woman in her mid-twenties who wore thick red lipstick, asked me if I'd like one more with a smile. I declined and asked for my check.

CHAPTER EIGHT

Two months later I was beginning to settle in to my new life. Work was going well, I was starting to find my way around better, and the dogs had stopped staring at me from the edge of the fence when I left or came home. They never barked. But since the first day I moved in, as I either got in or out of my car at the foot of the carriage house, they would be there, staring. I could feel their eyes on the back of my neck.

The routine that I found myself in was on the days that I worked. I would go out afterwards in the hopes of finding her. I know that it was ridiculous to think that in a major city with millions of people I would magically run into the one person that I hadn't seen in over twenty years and who might not be here in the first place. The lunacy of it was palpable. But I didn't know what else to do. I had to find her. I had to look at her and find out if what I felt all of those years ago was bullshit. That all of it was bullshit. I didn't want it to be, but a sinking feeling in the pit of my stomach every time I thought about why I was looking for Liberty, reduced my overall hope to a single point.

Usually I went out alone, not wanting to discuss the reason I went all over the city and always to a different place. Occasionally I would go out with a few of the servers, as long as they were going somewhere I hadn't been. But those nights were always filled with shop-talk and bitching. Sometimes it was nice to vent about a crappy table, but over the years I had learned to let that stuff go once I left the building for the night. Sitting around and listening to other people's bitching now raked at my nerves. On those nights, I ducked out after a drink and went somewhere else.

At least once a week over the last month I did go out for drinks after work with one other person. Mars, whose real name was Marschall, was one of the cooks at Stem. He was quiet at work. We didn't exchange a single word until I had been there for about three weeks. He was almost my height, a little above six feet, but he appeared taller than me because he was so thin. His head was shaved bald and he spoke with a thick urban southern.

The two of us had quite a bit in common. For one, we both loved rap. In the kitchen, each day, a different cook was allowed to choose the music that they listened to while they prepped during the afternoon. The music stayed on until service started at five, so most days when I went into the kitchen to grab a rack of washed glasses from the night before, music still filled the room, bouncing off of the copper pots and pans that hung from hooks. The first time he spoke to me was one of these afternoons. I walked into the kitchen and before the swinging, thin plastic door was all the way open, my head had already begun to nod. Nineties hip hop rushed out of a metal third pan, in which the kitchen's wireless speaker had been placed to create a magnified sound. Without thought I began to rap along with the music.

"What you know about this?" Mars' first words to me came from across the line.

"I know good music," I said back.

"A'ight then."

That moment sparked a friendship. In the weeks following, if I heard a new verse on a track, or a question that a fellow hip hop head would appreciate came to mind, I shared it with Mars. He and I also shared a love for basketball. We were both big Atlanta Hawks fans, which was more often than not a source of frustration and disappointment. But it was nice to have someone to bitch about those with. He was convinced that the team was cursed after they traded the franchise's best player of all time, Dominique Wilkens, when the team was in first place. I wasn't sure about a curse, but he wasn't the first person to share the same sentiment. 'Nique now did the commentary on television during games. As one of the most athletic players and dunkers the league has ever seen, I was convinced that he could still throw it down, even though most of his hair had grayed. Mars agreed.

The other reason why I tolerated Mars coming out for drinks over the rest of the staff was that while we had a lot to talk about, we didn't talk that much at all. He would seem to get as lost in his head as I did as we sat at the bar and sipped on our drinks. If you saw Mars walking towards you on the sidewalk, you would probably move out of his way. His arms covered in tattooed sleeves, his shaved head, and the perpetual glare he held in eyes like he was sizing everything in his path up, could be quite menacing. You definitely wouldn't think that he was one of the best cooks in the city. He worked the sauté station behind the line. Anything prepared in a stainless-steel pan warped from time spent sizzling over blue gas flames was his. Scallops, fish, foie gras, as well as all of the vegetables and sauces that accompanied the proteins on the plate were his responsibility.

"Cooking fish is an art. You know what I'm sayin'?" he said to me one night after we had been sitting quietly at a bar in downtown Decatur. "I mean, other shit has recipes. Like, there's a formula and shit. But every piece of fish is different. Even if I cut them the exact same way, they're still always a little different. You feel me?" I nodded back, sipping my martini. "It's a feelin'. That's all you got. You gotta actually touch it while it's in the pan, you know, to feel it, to see where it's at. But you've also got to have that gut feelin'. "Cause a piece of fish keeps cooking after you pull it off the heat. Know what I'm sayin'? To get it jus' right—to cook it perfect—you just got to have that feelin'. You don't know it's ready to pull it from the heat until it sounds right. It sounds crazy as shit what I'm sayin', but I'm for real. You can hear it." Then he was quiet again and neither of us said anything until highlights from the night in basketball came on the television behind the bar and some unlucky player got dunked on.

"Yo, George. Look at this shit!" he said to me.

"Damn," I responded. It was a nasty dunk. "I feel bad for that dude."

"Fo' sho'."

Then I was pulled back into my head and my gaze swept the room before going back to the door.

CHAPTER NINE

Most people think that waiting tables is easy. That all you have to do is take an order—correctly, mind you—and then keep everyone at their table happy. But that's the rub. Their table. They can't think beyond it. What about the other tables a server is responsible for? What about the multitude of other issues that are out of a server's control? No one who hasn't done the job actually realizes what it takes to pull it off. And the higher up you go in service—the better the caliber of restaurant—the harder it gets.

The skill set required at the highest level is akin to the skill set of professionals making ten times the money. It's all about the read. About subtle pushes and pulls. About understanding where the leverage is. As a rule, I only ask questions that I already know the answer to. And when I'm asked questions, my response is specific enough to satisfy, but vague enough not pigeon-hole myself. I've always got an out. I provide unsolicited information that covers my ass if something outside of my control goes sideways, and omit anything that might garner attention. The key to the whole thing is the first thirty seconds. If I haven't convinced the people at the table that I am a professional who's only priority is to make them happy, then I've already lost. Doubt of this will result in looking for issues moving forward rather than relaxing and allowing me to fade into the blurred background of the dining room.

The greatest irony of the restaurant business concerns understanding and appreciating what servers and bartenders bring to the table. Because surprisingly, one demographic who understands the least of what we do, is Chefs. They think that serving is easy. They have no idea of the nuance. Nuance only exists to describe their food. To be honest, not every Chef is this daft when it comes to the front of the house, just the vast majority if them. Especially the young ones. They think that because they waited tables one summer when they were twenty at some cookie cutter chain restaurant that they understand the entirety of what a professional server with a decade of experience does. In their minds they are artists. We are drones.

When I first got into fine dining the fact that this disparity of respect between the front and back of the house exists really pissed me off. But over the years I just came to expect it. I just treated the Chef like they were sitting at one of my tables. I asked the questions they wanted me to, I answered theirs with what they wanted to hear, and I took being condescended to by someone who didn't understand what I did with a grain of salt. The longer I stayed in the business, the funnier it became to hear a Chef actually talk about what we as servers do. It was like somewhere during culinary school they were all given the same pamphlet on what a server is. And instead of listing a set of skills like: emotionally intelligent, graceful, and able to multitask as well as prioritize a constantly changing list of duties, while under a tremendous amount of pressure, their pamphlet simply reads: "Servers have big personalities and love talking and taking care of other people." I can't count how many times a Chef has complimented a group of servers on their "big personalities." The level of insult is hard to describe. It would be similar to server school (which doesn't exist, and thank God) passing out their own pamphlet about Chefs that describes them as: "People who enjoy hot places and try not to burn shit."

The shame of it all is that I, as well as most of the servers I've worked with, really respect what a Chef is. We're impressed with the hours they put in (even though most would be considered text-book workaholics—something a server has never been and never will be), with their dedication to their craft; we respect it as an art. We appreciate the creativity and the subtlety. Even though they don't see the similarity, we respect the way every Chef demands that every plate that leaves their kitchen is perfect, just as we do the same with our tables when we set up the dining room before service. It's just a shame there isn't mutual respect the vast majority of the time. The chef at Stem was the rare exception. And there is no doubt in my mind that it was directly related to the white that had washed his hair completely years ago. As a young Chef, I'm sure he was like all the rest.

Chef Raymond didn't talk much. When he would come to line up to go over any changes on the menu he was soft spoken and to the point. In contrast to his age-ridden hair, his icy, bright blue eyes held the stoic stare of someone half his age. His intelligence was apparent yet somehow it seemed to wrap him in innocence. I found out from Trey that the owner was his life long friend and he trusted Chef Raymond with every decision. For all practicality, it was Chef's restaurant.

His food was as simple as the descriptions he gave about it. "Putting together fifteen ingredients isn't that hard," I heard him say to his Sous one day in the kitchen. "Three ingredients, executed perfectly, with no room for error—that's hard. All those other ingredients cover up flaws." What he was most known for in the culinary word was his soup. Soup to Chef was the ultimate representation of simplicity and grace in cooking. While the menu stayed for the most part the same for the current season—the accompaniments to some dishes changing as new veggies and fruit became available—Chef would change the soup at least once every week, sometimes more. There was only ever one on the menu however; yet the soup that was printed every day on the thick khaki paper seemed to be a reflection of the mood of Chef Raymond.

The first full week I spent at Stem, the soup was a vichyssoise, a classic composition of potato and leek, served chilled. After being formally introduced to him, Chef said barely a word to me, or anyone else for that matter. He seemed lost in himself. At war with something that tugged at his core. On more than one occasion, he called for "hands" in the kitchen—a signal to anyone qualified in the front of the house, be it a server assistant or general manager that food needed to be run—but when I repeated the call, letting him know that I was available, he seemed initially not to hear me. His gaze seemed pulled to the plates of food that sat on the stainless steel "pass," or counter that bridged the gap between the front and back of house. When a second or third person called back "hands," as they approached Chef, he bounced back out of his trance and called out where the food was to be run. "Scallop seat one, lady, pork, seat two—table twenty-six," he said to me as he shook his head slightly trying to pull himself completely back.

"Scallop one, lady, pork two," I echoed back, grabbing the two plates with black serviettes—folded linen napkins used to grasp the edge of the plates to both protect the hands of whoever ran the food in case the plate was hot, as well as, and probably more importantly, the plate from unsightly fingerprints. "Table twenty-six."

The following week the soup was a puree of sunchoke. Chef put up a bowl for the staff to try on Monday. While it looked thick and rich the off-white puree was surprisingly light and bright. The inherent sturdiness of the root was there, but only to provide structure. After swallowing the first spoon full, my mouth was left with the subtle yet firm taste of fresh lemon. It was absolutely amazing. That week Chef was more engaging than he had been before. A smile spread across his face and touched his eyes at least once every shift, if not more, regardless of how the day was going. I didn't think about the correlation with the soup until Maria pointed it out to me.

"It's wild, right?" she said, folding a loose piece of hair back behind her right ear. "I didn't believe it either when I first started. But sure enough, if you want to know the mood of the chef for the week, just look at what the soup is on Monday."

I thought for a long moment about what she was saying, trying to figure out if she was just jerking me around. "So is there a soup that we should be concerned about? I mean, is there one that means he's going to start firing people?" I said to her smartly.

Trey had been leaning on the server station, but hadn't said a word. "French onion," he said, still looking off into space, lost in his thoughts. He looked up at me. "If you see French onion on the menu, stay the fuck out of his way."

"French onion. Why French onion?" I said to them both.

"No one knows," Trey said, again letting his focus go back into a haze. "But feel free to ask him," he said with a sarcastic grin.

"I've never seen that soup before," Maria said pushing another loose hair behind her other ear. "But I've heard a few stories," she said with an exaggerated wink as she walked out of the server station and into the dining room.

"She's smarter than she lets on, right?" I said to Trey who still stared at nothing.

"Yup," he said as he pushed aside the dark brown heavy curtain and walked into the dining room himself.

This particular week, as the Georgia winter leaned as hard as it would all year, and threats of potential snow that would never come but would leave shelves of bottled water and canned goods naked for days, the soup was tomato. It was creamy and savory, but not in a way that didn't want for more. The bowl that it was served on was placed on a round plate with a cut up square of a previous menu keeping the former from sliding on the latter. On the right side of the plate that protruded from the bowl were two small triangles of butter grilled bread with cheddar cheese oozing ever so gently from their middles.

Chef attended line-up everyday. I was off Tuesday, but worked every other shift during the week. All week Chef hadn't said a word outside of going over the tomato soup on Monday afternoon. But Saturday, after Jim finished going over the changes in the wine pairings for the tasting menu, Chef Raymond stood up from the chair he had occupied in the shadowed corner of the room, and began to speak.

"I've spent decades in this business. One thing that I've learned is that the best food in the world can be ruined by bad service. A bad night—the worst night—in the kitchen, though, can be saved by good service. I appreciate what you do. And I thank you for it." I was floored. I had never heard a Chef utter words so. I left my seat and walked into the dining room with a sense of purpose that had been lacking for years. Respect from a source that never provided it soothed old wounds. Most nights before, when a Chef spoke about personalities and care, it took away from the impetus to be the best I could be that night; yet this night, when a Chef of all people recognized that we— that I—was more than a drone, it mattered.

CHAPTER TEN

I walked out of my childhood home and began to drive around the small town of Pensdale. While so many things seemed different as far as the look of the place, the feeling of it—it's soul—was the same. I wasn't really sure where I was going. I just needed to get away for awhile. So many memories flooding back like lava. Both the good and the bad melting into each other and becoming apart of the slow rolling mass that had been following me ever since I turned off of the highway; and ever so slowly gaining speed. I was hoping to find just one to cling onto. One that wouldn't burn too much. In hopes of staving off the eventuality of being totally consumed.

After almost circling the town, I found myself at the entrance of a park. It looked smaller than it had when I was in high school. This was the park where juniors and seniors once a month would sneak a keg into one of the large, metal trash cans in close proximity to the wooden pavilion that had been erected in the back right corner of the park, sharing a wall with the cemetery that had been there since the Civil War. A walk that years before had been filled with youthful anticipation, brought me quickly to that same pavilion. While many other aesthetics of the town had improved, the wooden structure looked exactly as it should have after twenty years, faded into a hue of tan with splinters sticking jaggedly out of the four main corner posts. The trash cans looked as though they hadn't been replaced either. It had stopped raining shortly after I left my parents' house. But the sky still held a weighty darkness.

I picked up a pine cone and tossed it at the rusty metal trash can farthest from me. I missed. I walked over slowly to one of the picnic tables and sat down, my legs resting on the wooden bench, and looked at the wall that separated me from so many gravestones. I thought about the last time I looked at that wall. Moss, thick and dark green had grown over the edge then. Now the moss had been stripped off, but the the outline of where it had been was still visible. Just barely. I thought about how Liberty had stood on that wall. And Arthur.

Arthur lived with his grandmother. She was old and mean, and was the last living relative that he had: Ida May. He spent as many nights at my mother's dinner table as he did at his grandmother's, if not more. By our freshman year in high school we were almost the same height. I had him by a half an inch, but I slumped. Most students in our class would have said he was taller. Had we been wearing hats, most people would have thought us brothers. We both had fair skin, were taller than average, and had blue eyes. But hats removed we stood apart. My hair was dark brown, almost black, and stringy at best. His was blond—no…golden. He was my best friend.

In rural Georgia in the early nineteen nineties, middle school had yet to be invented. Instead of bridging the gap between elementary and high school, children were forced to dive headfirst into the frosted waters of the latter, and barely able to catch their breath. The kings and queens who had ruled justly over their child subjects, now became the jesters of an older court—forced to dance awkwardly in circles, simultaneously trying to impress their new masters while avoiding punishment. It was a rite of passage that was both feared and lusted after. And once the metamorphosis was complete, childhood was left behind for good, leaving in its wake, a trail of innocence.

Arthur was what every teenage boy wanted to be. Charm oozed from him like sweat and awkwardness from the rest of us. And every girl his age as well as more than a few that were older orbited him like love-drunk satellites. But that's the rub. We couldn't be him. Because he really wasn't real. Or at least you weren't completely sure the first time you met him. Like Phineas.

I was always to follow Arthur socially. Alone I fought him as an equal, but in the whirlpool of high school politics, I let him lead. It was easier that way. I wasn't that bad of an athlete myself. More than once I beat him at the elementary school court down the street from our house in a game of one on one. But I didn't have that connection that he had. They were pulled to him: The lights. When they shone bright I felt doubt. He felt strength. Like those photons raining down upon and around him in both waves and points gave him some kind of power. We were inseparable. But then everything changed. All it took was one day. The day that Arthur first saw her. The day that he found me at my locker after the final bell and told me all about her. About Liberty.

Liberty Scott moved to Pensdale shortly after Christmas break of our eighth grade year. On the mile walk from school to my house Arthur enthusiastically told me everything that he knew about her. Which wasn't much aside from that she had moved to our small town from Atlanta and that she wasn't very happy about it.

"She's the most beautiful thing I've ever seen," he said as he looked up towards the bright blue sky brushed with a few whips of white. Arthur was prone to being a little dramatic. But coming from him, most people ate it up.

"Oh yeah? Well, what does she look like?"

"Like an angel."

"Oh. An angel. I can see her now," I said back sarcastically.

He stopped walking and turned around to face me. "She's got the prettiest smile I've ever seen, George. She's got brown hair and she's kinda short. Not too short, like cute short. I'm telling you, an angel. You'll see George," he said as he spun back around took a few quick steps and then leaped and hung from a low branch that reached over the edge of the sidewalk.

"So how'd you meet her anyway," I said as he let go and dropped back down.

"I didn't tell you?" I shook my head. "Oh. Well. You know that big tree in front of the school—the one close to the road?" This time I nodded. "Well I was running to science after lunch 'cause I knew the bell was about to ring and then it did. So I stopped running 'cause I was late already. And that's when I saw her. She was running. Well not really running as much as walking as fast as she could. She came from behind that tree. The one next to the road. But then she dropped something. A notebook. A green notebook. I guess she didn't realize her backpack wasn't all the way zipped. So I ran over and grabbed it. I caught up to her right as she reached the door to the North building."

"And then what?"

"She said thanks and then went inside." I looked at him confused. "Oh. So I went to class—science—which is in the East. But then I ran back after class and waited for her to come back out. And then she did. When I went up to her she looked at me all weird, like I was on fire or something and then she walked away. I saw that her bag wasn't closed again and that that green notebook was kinda sticking out, so I grabbed it."

"You grabbed it?"

"Yeah. And then I hopped in front of her and handed it back. I told her she dropped it again. At first she seemed pissed. But then she smiled." Only Arthur. If I had grabbed a notebook out of some girl's bag I would have gotten a slap in the face for sure. "I introduced myself and then she told me her name. Then I walked her back to the East building and we talked."

"And you haven't seen her since."

"No. But I'm going to go and look behind that tree tomorrow at lunch." Which is exactly what he did. After school the next day as I stood in the same place in front of my locker I as I had the day before, Arthur tapped me on my shoulder. "George, this is Liberty." I turned around. Standing next to Arthur was a girl with shoulder length brown hair, the front of which fell on half of her freckled face. She ran her right hand over her forehead and through her dark brown locks exposing her face entirely for a moment before it fell back down exactly as it had before. I stared at her. She wore an open green flannel with a gray t-shirt underneath, faded blue jeans, and green Pumas. A maroon backpack hung from her left shoulder. Although she had only made brief eye contact with me as she waved hello before looking back at Arthur and then adjusting the strap on her shoulder, there was a depth to her green eyes that I would never forget.

"I'm gonna walk her home," Arthur said to me as he turned towards the doorway at the other end of the hall. "I'll come over after. Cool?"

"Yeah, cool," I responded as the two of them walked away through the throng of bustling students. I stood and watched them walk away from me. I watched her walk away all the way to the large double doors that led outside. Arthur almost bounced as he navigated the others around him, saying hellos and giving and receiving high fives. She seemed to be focusing more on the tiled floor than on the people around her. As they entered the threshold together, Arthur grabbed her hand.

I didn't remember walking home that afternoon. The thought of her consumed the entirety of my focus. Arthur was right. She was absolutely beautiful. Even though I didn't even speak to her, butterflies filled my gut, and warmth my chest, as my mind tried desperately but futilely to push away any thought of her hand in Arthur's, not mine.

As I turned away from the wall of the cemetery and began walking back to my car—vivid memories swirling in my head—I wondered if that feeling I had that day was real at all. To believe that I was in love after a thirty second encounter. That every other girl in my school was now blurred. Or was it a manifestation of youth that would have happened eventually whether I met Liberty at all? In eighth grade having a girlfriend was like having a six figure income at thirty. And in the scheme of things, held about as much importance in regards to one's actual happiness. The idea—the symbolism—held greater weight than the reality. But two decades later, real or not, I could still feel the subtle echo of those butterflies when I thought about her. I laid in my childhood bed that night only able to hold on to a few hours of sleep before morning began to creep through the blinds and a visit to Liberty's house to see her mother became that much more real with every tick of light that passed.

CHAPTER ELEVEN

Pairing is by far my favorite aspect of wine. The rest of it kind of bores me to be honest. But the perfect pairing—one that has comparative and contrastive qualities—becomes more than just the sum of its parts. I heard it described once as "one plus one equals three." Amen. I can understand why someone might choose the holistic study of wine as a career, though. The amount of dedication, knowledge, and passion needed to really grasp the entire process is quite impressive—daunting really.

When a new wine pairing was discussed at line up, Jim's face would light up more than any other time that night. He loved all of it. He would first go over the pairing itself—why the wine worked with the dish. His rationale was usually quite simple. "Think of the bright lemony acidity of this wine as the squeeze of lemon over the fish itself," he said one day. The dish in question was the third course on the tasting menu that night, a pan roasted grouper served over a cauliflower puree, accompanied by sautéed artichokes, and a lemon gastrique. A gastrique is a sauce made by cooking down vinegar and sugar along with whatever other flavors are wanted, usually incorporated into a dish to provide acid. The bottle of wine that Jim held against his left palm—his middle and ring finger supporting the base of it, pressed inside the rounded divot, or "punt," while the pointer and middle finger of his right hand supported gently the glass neck, was a Spanish wine, from the Basque region specifically—Txakoli to be exact—the "tx" producing a "ch" sound in this part of the world—and the grape was hondoribi zuri. "You should remember this producer," he said as he held the bottle, label facing towards us, reverently. "We carried their rose last year. It was a blend of the other grape grown in this region. The red varietal. Does anyone remember it's name?" Silence. "I'm so happy to see that you've all retained so much knowledge," he intoned in the manner of a British butler, and with the same look of disdain in contrast to the smile that spread like chunky peanut butter across his face. "Hondaribi beltza is what one of you must have muttered under your breath," he said through his smile. "Otherwise I'd look like a fool standing here talking to myself." The bit of tension that began growing when he first asked the question was dispelled with a wink and then the placement of the bottle on the wooden table. Jim then pulled out his wine key, opened the bottle quickly, yet softly, and then poured a small taste into the cluster of glasses that rested on the table in front of him. "What do you smell?" he asked, after the glasses had been distributed.

I figured if I got involved early I could keep quiet for the rest of lineup. The easiest answer would of course be lemon, but knowing Jim, that would earn a stern look as that was the only descriptor he'd already provided. "The lemon is there for sure, but I also get something a little rounder." I spoke up first.

"Okay, I like that, George. Like what?"

I racked my brain trying to match the subtle, secondary aroma to something more tangible than a shape as Jim's gaze focused on me. Then it clicked. "Round, yet almost a little sweet. Like elderflower."

Jim beamed as he turned his focus to someone else in the room. "Very good, George. I think you hit the nail right on the head." I got lucky. The night before a very obnoxious woman must have ordered six cocktails made with elderflower liqueur and sparkling wine. The smell of the drink, while not overly pungent, cut through the rest of the aromas in the dining room each time I brought another to the table. I leaned back in my chair with the thought of a smile, knowing that I would be free of scrutiny for the duration of line up. It wasn't that Jim was overly critical or there were overt consequences if one of us couldn't answer a question, I just really wasn't in the mood to interact with anyone at all. I wouldn't have a choice as soon as my first table sat down, so until then, I wanted to keep to myself as much as possible.

That feeling—not wanting to interact with people unless necessary—had been a constant ever since I arrived at Stem. I had never been anything close to an extrovert, but in the past was able to enjoy social banter. But now it held no appeal for me at all. It was as though my desire to find Liberty was pushing me further into myself. I still had drinks with Mars, but about half of the time neither one of us spoke more than five words to each other. Tableside I was always able to turn on my engaging personality if I had to, but loathed every second of it. I preferred a business table that wanted me to be seen and not heard. I could focus on the minutia—get lost for a while in creating an experience where the guests at my table never had to look around in want, but never really noticed I was there.

But then there were the other tables. The ones that wanted to act like my friend. As a general rule I never introduced myself when I greeted a table. There was no need. What my name was had nothing to do with my ability to do my job. Some servers immediately told their tables their name, usually in hopes of creating a connection and then receiving a bigger tip. What they didn't realize it that usually it came across as gauche. They also didn't realize that for the most part, the tip that you are going to receive from any given table is based strictly on how they always tip. You could introduce yourself, create a rapport, and banter with a table as much as you like, but if as a rule they don't tip on wine, they're not going to change that tonight, just because you told them your name, followed later in the evening with a story about your dog.

A few weeks later my first table of the night was a party of three men in their fifties. My shoulders slumped and the possibility of a smile looking anything more than forced went away when I noticed that each of them was unzipping a leather wine bag as I approached. They were seated at a table usually reserved for five or six and I realized why as I reached the table and each of them had pulled out two bottles. Normally this would have been Thomas' table. He loved schmoozing with the wine elite in hopes of getting to taste what they brought in. But Thomas was on vacation.

"Well, I think that we should decide what we're eating first before we choose which bottles to open," the guy to my immediate right said as I began placing down menus. He was the oldest looking of the three—his almost completely gray hair that surrounded a shining bald spot on the top of his head pulled together into a tight and short ponytail.

"Of course," the guy seated across from him replied as though what he had said was a known fact. His hair was full, but cut short, and a dark bushy beard fell from his face like Brillo.

"I do have to say," the third man said, "that regardless, we must open the DRC." The other two men nodded with similar expressions on their faces—their brows furrowed as though deep in thought and their lips pursed as though they were trying to represent aces as far as the quality of what they were going to say next. Neither of the three men had acknowledged me whatsoever.

"Good evening, gentlemen," I said with a pinched smile. The three of them each said one more thing to the collective before looking towards me—the expressions on their face betraying the thought that whatever it was I had to say, paled in comparison. But I didn't give a shit. I just wanted to get this over with. "Are you all familiar with our menu?" I said, my eyes squinting with as much pain as my smile. They looked at each other for a few seconds before the one with the ponytail responded.

"Well, I've eaten here before, but I suppose you could go over it. So that we can decide which bottles to open. And just to let you know, we'll definitely need some white wine glasses for champagne. We'll be starting with the vintage Krug."

"Absolutely," I said, before going over the menu in extensive detail, watching with sadistic pleasure the looks on their faces as they waited for me to finish and go and get their glasses. That was why they were here after all. Not for the food, or the service—but to be able to pull out their wine cocks and claim to have the biggest. Usually, the value of the bottle held sway when it came to who was the winner, but with a group like this, other factors could weigh in. The "DRC," or Domaine de la Romanee-Conti, could be worth as much as twenty-five grand depending on the year and vineyard, so the guy swinging that one was most likely in the lead. After I finished explaining everything, I presented the wine list out of spite. They politely declined with eyes now squinting as much as mine. I grabbed three white wine glasses, leisurely, and returned to the table. The three of them were pouring over the menu and debating which of the bottles would pair best with each dish. I presented the bottle of champagne which Jim had placed in a nearby ice bucket. After I cut the foil and began to loosen the cork, all three of them looked up from their menus. When I removed the cork with only the slightest hiss, they nodded, almost in unison, before continuing to ignore me as I poured a taste for the one who had asked for the glasses. He swirled the heavy taste of wine twice, before sticking in his bulbous nose and inhaling deeper than he needed to.

"It's fine," he said, placing the glass back on the table, without taking a sip, and held his shoulders with a squareness of pride as though he just climbed a mountain. It wasn't that hard to tell that a bottle was intact by just the nose. I poured half glasses of champagne for the other two before I did the same for the taster. I placed the bottle back into the metal wine bucket filled three quarters of the way with ice a few feet away and then addressed the table once more. As I began to speak and offer to return in a few minutes, I was cut off by the ponytail and asked to do just that. I walked away without responding. I knew exactly what these guys wanted, yet they refused to allow me to provide it without feeling the need to guide me along like I was blind. The worst part was the condescending smiles. As though I should be thanking them for being so kind as to educate me on the finer points of wine and service. It was only my fucking job. Did I show up at their places of work and talk to them like they didn't know what they were doing, only to have them thank me for it? Nope.

I walked away quickly and didn't return for at least ten minutes. As I approached the table—apparent that I was heading directly towards my three favorite guys—ponytail met my gaze and then motioned me over. "Yes."

"We are all set, young man."

"Very good."

"So what we'd like to do, if it's possible…" the guy with the bushy beard said, knowing completely well that it was. "…is to order a few courses to pair with some wine and then share them. Is that possible?"

"Absolutely," I said back. "I can split items if you like for the table, or bring share plates; whichever you prefer."

"Oh, just bring plates. There's no reason to split the dishes. I wouldn't want to ruin the presentation," ponytail said with a smirk. He had brought the DRC and was trying to run the show. He proceeded to order for the group as well as tell me in which order they'd like the bottles of wine opened, as well as which glass (as if it wasn't my job to know) to pour them in. The wine they had was spectacular. And they, or maybe it was ponytail, ordered the wrong food. But I played along anyway as though they hadn't. After the champagne they wanted to start with mushroom and goat cheese toast on ciabatta, grilled octopus with a Spanish romesco sauce, and seared foie gras with candied apples. The wine they wanted open was a white Burgundy—a Meursault, Grand Cru. Yeah, the apples on the foie worked with the wine, but not much else. For the second course, to pair with the DRC, they ordered the breast of duck and the trout. Not bad choices, but mushrooms and French pinot sing. The ciabatta from the first course would have paired better. But even more so, the guinea hen with chanterelles and dried cherries would have been perfect. The wine was so good, they wouldn't for a moment think that their meal could be better. But it could. The final course, paired with a St. Emillion, was the short rib and the lamb chop. This was by far the best paired course as the rich, dark fruit of the merlot with its mellowed tannin worked beautifully with both meats. But the three men only spoke about the wine while they ate their final savory course. It wasn't as good as the previous vintage apparently, and then the conversation quickly switched to a bottle that ponytail had drank the week before. Half of the beef and lamb still sat decadently on their respective plates when I was summoned over again to clear the table.

They declined dessert, not having brought an appropriate wine. I'm not sure whether it was a mistake by one of the three or intentional. They finished the Bordeaux and then ordered double espressos. By the time they finished the coffee, they were the last table in the restaurant and had been for at least thirty minutes. I cleared the small, white espresso cups as well as the white rectangular caddie filled with different types of powdered sweetener. Including the twenty five-dollar corkage fee for each bottle, their check came to just under three hundred dollars. I dropped it in the middle of the table and ponytail quickly grabbed it to my dismay. Out of the three, he seemed the most entitled—the least likely to realize how much work I had actually done outside of normal dining. Ninety-nine times out of a hundred my read was right. But not this time. Left me one fifty.

CHAPTER TWELVE

I went to college to study music. It was my passion. The way that I felt I could relate to the rest of the world. Maybe my way of escaping from it. And I let it consume me. I was constantly in the practice room; never seen around campus without my horn. By the end of my freshman year I had positioned myself to be one of the better trumpet players in school when I returned the following fall. That summer however, I allowed my art to consume me in a different way. Hubris. I spent the first week of summer break doing exactly as I had since I arrived at school. I practiced and practiced until the corners of my mouth burned and my fingers felt unnatural if not pressing down on oiled keys. But then something happened.

A classmate asked me if I could fill in for him at a gig. A wedding. The thought hadn't crossed my mind that I was ready to make money with music, but I accepted anyway. It was easy. I played the Trumpet Voluntary—a piece I had memorized in tenth grade. It went well. Very well. I already had a tux from playing in the concert band and orchestra, so all I really had to do was show up and play. After the ceremony the wedding planner—the older sister of the bride—handed me an envelope and thanked me profusely, telling me how amazingly I played and how it made the wedding that much more beautiful. I thanked her gracefully and left. I opened the envelope when I buckled the seatbelt to my '85 Chevy Cavalier and was shocked to see a check for two hundred dollars. My classmate reached out and thanked me for filling in for him and I told him that I would be happy to do it any time. He chuckled and said that he'd keep me in mind. But the feeling of that check in my hands from doing the thing that I loved more in the world than anything wouldn't leave me.

A couple weeks later I was playing scales late at night, where usually I had the place to myself, and I heard laughter coming down the practice hall towards me. Normally I would have ignored it, but I didn't. I poked my head out of the small room lined with thick cork and saw three people walking towards me. They seemed excited. The kind of excited that can only happen to people under the age of twenty-five and after midnight, but had nothing to do with drugs or booze. It was the elation of an idea, usually shared, that made you feel like your life was about to change. Ninety-nine percent of the time it absolutely did not, but you thought it would. And somehow by opening that door I unknowingly became sucked into theirs.

The band that we formed consisted of Juliette, a petite brunette with huge brown eyes, who sang soprano at school, Luke, a classical guitarist who was terribly skinny yet had the bushiest sideburns I had ever seen, myself, and Max, a piano player, who was the oldest of the four of us—a senior in the fall—and the one whose idea it had been in the first place that pulled the rest of us in. Max and Juliette were both go-getters and we had a gig to play at a local dive bar two weeks later. It didn't go great, but it somehow led to a second try playing blues with a dash of classical panache. Juliette, when performing classical, had quite a clear and poignant timbre to her voice, but in our band she sang with innocent rasp.

By the time fall semester rolled around we had played four times in three different venues. While my goal was still Carnegie Hall, my focus was not nearly as sharp as it had been before. Instead of first chair, I played third. Still first trumpet. But the third chair. I was better than the other two in front of me, but the idea and feeling of playing my own music trumped the scales and etudes that before had consumed me. When Christmas break rolled around, Max approached the three of us with a proposition.

"We should go on tour," he said across the table at The Blarney Stone, an Irish pub just off campus, to Luke and me, his left arm draped around Juliette. The two of them recently started dating.

"We definitely should," she said with vigor and hope in her doe eyes. "We've started gaining momentum in the last few months. Max—"

"I've found us some other gigs. A bunch of them. But they're not in town. We'd need to travel for a while. Go on the road!" he said, pulling Juliette closer. He held the same look in his eyes as Juliette. High on life and delusion—the product of youth and hours watching Saved by the Bell. The American dream. I looked at Luke to my right.

"I'm in," he said, the same glaze quickly covering his eyes. "I'm in!" he said slapping Max's outstretched right hand. He then looked at me. "What about you, George? You in?"

My father's favorite quote is a Chinese proverb: "Youth is wasted on the young." He must have muttered that under his breath thousands of times during my time at home. Had I thought for at least five minutes on what it actually might mean I may not have immediately blurted out, "Me too!" I gave Max the same high five and then he went to the bar and ordered shots. You couldn't get served at "The Blarney" without an ID, but once drinks were paid for they didn't seem to care who drank them.

I decided to wait until our inevitable success to tell my parents that I wasn't going to return for my second semester of my sophomore year. In fact, the first day that classes resumed after winter break, the four of us were in Max's Volvo station wagon, heading towards the coast to our first gig. The next night we played in front of about eighteen people, most of whom were more focused on their drinks than on us. We sounded great. The energy that had started in the booth weeks earlier was still with us. As we packed up that night however, that energy had begun to fade, at least for me and Luke. Juliette and Max still buzzed and assured us, after Max got free shots from the bar, that big things were still to come. Luke and I let him pull us back in.

A month later Max and Juliette broke up. She went straight home and the three of us remaining decided to part ways. Luke was going home to to beg his parents' forgiveness and swear to get back to school. Max wasn't sure what he was going to do, but I figured he'd go back as well, seeing as he was close to a degree. I probably should have as well, but I didn't. I ended up in Savannah chasing the fantasy of playing music for a living. My classical chops had gotten sloppy, but I found a richer tone in my horn that hadn't been there before. I played a few solo gigs here and there, hoping to draw the attention of anyone really, but money, what I had left from my grandparents college fund that they had set up the day after I was born, was almost gone.

I took a job waiting tables at a sports bar a few nights a week to supplement what little I was making playing. The job came to me easily. I always had good balance and a sense of efficiency. And while I would never say that I was an extrovert, I learned very quickly to read the bar goers that sat in my section. Once I figured out what they wanted from me, I gave it to them. And it was fun. I got to watch sports all night as I slung shots, beers, and every type of fried food imaginable. When I got off, I would hang around and have a few drinks myself. When I was hired, the manager of the place, a rectangular blond woman at the edge of fifty never asked me for my driver's license. I was six months away from my twentieth birthday, but I drank at the bar every night.

As time went by, I worked more and played less. I found a room for rent about a mile from the restaurant shortly after I got hired. It was a basement apartment and the people who owned the house were at work during the day so I could practice without bothering anyone. I still told myself every morning that I would find another gig, or at least an open mic, but by the end of most days I was more focused on drinking and trying to get laid. Part time quickly turned into full time. A year later I realized I hadn't even taken out my trumpet in a month. I convinced myself I needed a fresh start and decided to move somewhere else where my music would take more precedence in my life. Another year later I moved again, still stuck in the same rut of waiting tables, partying, and then getting up again the next day and doing it all over again. I still played, but it was more to try and keep up my chops than anything else.

The restaurant business is a fickle mistress. You feel the whole time like it's a means to an end. A temporary solution that allows you to also do what you really want. It's enough money to keep the bills paid and still have fun. The schedule is flexible so you have time to do the things that you are certain are going to finally get you to the place that you've been moving towards the entire time. You're so close. Always so close. But somehow only a rare few of us actually break through. The rest end up in one of Zeno's paradoxes, convinced that they are that much closer to their ultimate goal, never grasping that they can't actually ever get there if they continue on the same path. And then years have passed, decades, and there really isn't anything else that a career server is qualified to do. Even though you have a set of skills that is prized in many fields: the ability to read people, to make quick and precise decisions while constantly prioritizing an entirely separate list of other tasks that have to be accomplished, or being comfortable talking to anyone, especially wealthy people who are accustomed to getting their way—it's futile. That's the rub. A server whose extremely good at their job doesn't actually appear to be doing that much at all. An employer looking at your resume and seeing only restaurant experience isn't going to think you could possibly understand advertising. So even though you thought that you'd finally gotten out, there you are again the next day promising yourself that this time next year—the same promise you've made every year since the beginning—you'd finally get there. And as the years pass and your skills develop more and more, you never realize that the way that you've learned to con the people at your tables—convincing them of their importance so that they relax and miss the little things that haven't gone their way, so that they order another bottle of wine—that you've been doing it to yourself the entire time.

CHAPTER THIRTEEN

The fall of 1996 began eight days early, on September 13. I didn't understand that day, sitting at my desk in Spanish class—the air around me heavy with tears—looking over the head of my teacher at the generic black and white clock that had been on every wall of every classroom I'd ever been in—at the red second hand clicking—what really had happened. We had already lost Kurt. Now 'Pac? It was the beginning—the beginning of losing ourselves, just like they had along with Morrison and Hendrix, what seemed like a lifetime ago.

The bell rang. I didn't move. I sat there, feeling, as the rest of the class pushed towards the door. After a long moment I got up and walked slowly through the halls. A girl stared at me as I passed by. Her blue eyes were wet. Her cheeks red. She looked at me like I had some answer to a question she couldn't let go. But I didn't. The second bell rang. I kept my pace until I reached the music building. "Ah, Mr. Muirhill, nice of you to join us," Mr. Goodwin, the orchestra teacher announced to the rest of class, keeping his eyes on the score lying upon his podium. He wore the same neon orange fisherman's hat that always perched upon his head and his gray beard had grown nearly to his chest. "Take your seat." As I passed the podium on my way to my chair he shot me a glance and shook his head. I sat down and dove into myself; not into my emotions, or even into my thoughts, but into my memories—a bastardization of them both. I closed my eyes.

"Music, has nothing to do with notes," Mr. Goodwin spoke, placing his baton on the podium in front of him. "It is alive. The notes on the pieces of paper in front of you are dead. The person who wrote them is dead. Your instruments are dead. Now, you can pick them up and you can look at the notes on the page and play the right ones, at the right time, even in tune, but they are still dead. You all probably think that when you play these notes—these dead notes—that you are giving them life. You're wrong. You're not. Music has nothing to do with notes. In fact, I would go as far to say that music—real music—what people both live and die for, has nothing to do with sound at all. The real music, the thing that reaches out and grabs your heart, exists outside of notes...outside of instruments...outside of sound itself. It exists in the silence—in the moment that becomes you when you're pulled into it, making you wait just a fraction of a second longer than you are supposed to before you play the note, because it just doesn't feel right. And when you do this, then the notes become alive. They are no longer bound to page. They are free. And you are free along with them. Don't waste your time distracted by the notes that you see in front of you. They are dead. Pay attention to the space between them—to the silence—that is where the life is." His words followed me for the rest of the day—the irony of them leaving me in a haze.

It wasn't until I was walking to the band room shortly after the last bell rang to get my trumpet out of the instrument closet that the world seemed to come somewhat back into focus. My fingers on the metal door handle of the small hallway that led to the band hall, I heard a voice behind me. "George," Liberty said, walking quickly towards me. "Wait up."

"Hey, Liberty. What's up?"

"Look. I mean. Are you busy right now?"

"Not really."

"I mean, Arthur has practice. And... And I really don't want to be alone right now."

"Okay," I responded, confused. Liberty was now one of the most popular girls in school. The quarterback's girlfriend. She had changed since the end of the previous year. And so had Arthur. He was the starting quarterback now and in a small southern town like Pensdale there was no better place to be. I guess you could say that we were still friends. Kind of. The girl that I couldn't keep out of my mind because she was different, now stood before me as one of the rest of them. Even though her jeans had been cut into tight shorts and her t-shirt shrunk down a size, revealing both cleavage and her belly button, she dulled in comparison.

"Can we just hang out for a while?" she said. I looked at her more closely than before and saw that the edges of her eyes were red from crying.

"Yeah. Sure. What do you want to do?" I let go of the handle leaving my instrument at school for the night.

"Let's just drive for a while."

Fifteen minutes later we turned onto a slim dirt road that I wouldn't have noticed if we hadn't slowed down. It carved a path through the woods, mostly pine, their needles a brown carpet on the forest floor. A few hundred yards into the trees, Liberty pulled over onto the worn, dirt shoulder. "I want to show you something" she said. She grabbed my hand as soon as I was out of the car and pushed the metal door closed behind me with her foot. Her skin was soft. She pulled me through the woods at a half-run, dodging trees. A clearing opened. A pond the size of a large swimming pool was nestled cozily in the back right corner of the small field that lay before me. The grass, at least two feet high, had started to brown, but tiny purple and white buds clung still to the tops of scattered clumps of stalks. The edge of the pond was surrounded by patches of cattails, their long, blade like leaves stretching six feet in the air. What caught my gaze and held it, was a large willow tree that grew on the left bank and held its weeping branches only a few feet above the water.

Liberty let go of my hand and began to walk towards the pond. Her gait was slow, purposeful. I followed. When she reached the edge of the pond, the willow tree a few steps to her left, she turned her head towards me and smiled. But her eyes were as sad as they had been before. The first descent of Pachelbel played with slow and reverent fingers on weighted black and white keys.

She walked over to the tree and sat down, resting her back against the trunk. We sat in silence for a while watching the ripples gently in the fall breeze, as the melody in my head continued.

"George?"

"Yeah?"

"Do you think I'm pretty?" I froze. I stared at the pond straining to see its bottom through the murk. "Never mind. I'm being silly. Sorry."

"Of course I think you're pretty." I pulled my gaze towards her.

"You do…really?"

"Yeah. Definitely. You're beautiful."

She looked away with a smile and closed her eyes, holding on to the moment. "Thanks, George. George… there's a reason I wanted to talk to you," she said, looking at me once more.

"Okay. Sure."

"I don't know what to do," she said, as the beginnings of tears began to pool.

"What is it?"

She paused and wiped her eyes, looking away at the pond again. "I don't like who I'm becoming."

"What do you mean?" The notes of the Canon now building.

"I mean, I think I liked myself better before every girl in the school wanted to be friends with me. It's like I have to play some part now. As soon as school ended last year everyone knew that Arthur was going to be the starter this fall. This past summer has been surreal. Like a dream. A dream I wish I could wake up from. I mean I love Arthur. But he's different now too. When it's just the two of us, it's like it was in the beginning. But as soon as we're around anyone, he changes. He plays a part too. But it doesn't seem like it bothers him. That's why I wanted to talk to you, George. You're the only person who I thought might understand. You're different than the rest of them. You're not phony. I think about who I used to be and who I thought I would become. I was standing at my locker today after the the last bell and I looked down at my hands. I couldn't stop staring at them. Like they were someone else's. I don't wear pink glitter nail polish. I don't even wear nail polish. But there they were. I lost it. I ran into the trees behind the catwalk and couldn't stop crying. But then I saw you walking. And I just needed to be around someone who doesn't just see me as Arthur's girlfriend. We're friends, aren't we, George?" I looked back at her. Her focus had shifted back towards me with the question and I just stared back trying to process. "I mean I know we don't spend time together like we used to—the three of us. But I hope that we're still friends." Tears formed again in her green eyes and she let them fall down her cheeks as she looked at me waiting for me to respond.

"Of course we're friends." She looked at me with tears still hanging on her cheeks and the sadness left her eyes for the first time. The next thing I knew she had her arms wrapped around me. The simple melody only minutes earlier had now built upon itself, still slow in pace, but more complex, rising and falling with simplicity and depth. I held onto her. And for just a moment let myself believe that this wasn't just because she needed to feel better about herself. That maybe she would realize that it was me that she wanted, not Arthur. Then she pulled back and looked at me again. Her eyes shining.

And then she kissed me.

She pulled back slowly. The look in her eyes now fear. She put her hand over her mouth as she scooted away from me on the grass. The music stopped. "Come on let's go, she said quickly, looking away from me as she stood up. "I have to go pick up Arthur from practice."

Nothing was said in the car ride back to school. The warmth that washed over me in that moment had now turned cold and hard and sat in the pit of my stomach. At the light a block from campus, I said quickly that I would get out and didn't wait for a response before opening the door and hopping out onto the sidewalk. I knew what Liberty had meant about life feeling surreal as I walked slowly home.

The next day at school I saw her with a group of girls down the hallway as I stood at my locker. As the flock approached me I turned half away so as not to seem like I was trying to get her attention, but could still see her out of the corner of my eye. She walked past without looking towards me at all. I noticed however, that the nails on her right hand were no longer painted with pink polish. They were green, the same shade as her Pumas.

CHAPTER FOURTEEN

Two weeks later standing in the same spot, I found a folded piece of paper when I opened my locker before the first bell. A note from Liberty was written in neat cursive asking me to meet her after school. I felt anxious about seeing her again alone. A part of me had been trying to convince myself that things had changed. That she did have feelings for me now and was just trying to find the best way to tell Arthur. But the rest of me knew that that was ridiculous. She probably just wanted to make sure that I hadn't or wasn't going to say anything to him.

We met at a small park about a half mile from school. She was sitting in one of the swings when I arrived. "George," she said as a smile spread across her face. "Thanks for coming. I wasn't sure if you would."

"Okay," I said, surprised to see her so happy.

"Look, George. I, well, first, I wanted to say that I really value you as a friend. I mean you are really great to talk to and I think you really see me for who I am."

"Okay... Thanks," I said still trying to figure out the reason for her wanting to meet me.

"I mean you really helped me the other day. You helped me feel like I was still the person that I used to be—who I want to be. I hope we can still hang out sometime. Can we, George?"

"Yeah, sure. We can hang out," I said with slight hesitation.

"That's great. That's really great," she said standing up from the swing and closing the five feet that had separated us, opening her arms and then hugging me tightly. "'Cause I would really be disappointed if you didn't want to be my friend."

"Why wouldn't I want to be your friend?"

"Because of what I did. I kissed you. I mean I'm dating your best friend and I cheated on him. I didn't even realize it until it happened. But I still cheated on him. I was worried you might hate me. But Arthur never said anything so I guessed that you never told him. You haven't told him, have you?" she said as she let me go and took a step back towards the swings.

"No."

"And you're not going to?"

"No. Look. It's not like anything is going on between us," I said as the same knot formed in my stomach as on the ride back from the pond. "There's no need to hurt him if it didn't mean anything anyway." I knew that last part was manipulative. I wanted to see her reaction.

"It did mean something, George," she said smiling at me again. "I felt really close to you after you listened to me. It just can't happen again. I love Arthur."

I was shocked. I was certain that she was going to follow my lead and say that it didn't mean anything. I thought I had given her the out that she wanted. But she didn't take it. "It can't," I said back with false resoluteness. She hugged me again quickly before darting off towards her car. I wanted to call her back. I wanted to look her in the eyes and ask her why her nails were still painted. Ask her how she could open up to me about how she didn't like who she was becoming and then go right back to being that person. I wanted to tell her that it meant something to me too. It meant everything. But I didn't. I watched her get into her car and then drive away.

As time wore on, having gone to different bars scattered around metro Atlanta for the better part of six months, usually alone, I decided that maybe my plan had been flawed from the beginning. Instead of going randomly to different places hoping to cross paths with her, if I stayed in one place, the likelihood that I would be there when Liberty eventually walked through the door would be much higher. There were fewer moving parts I told myself. Mars was partial to a bar not too far from the restaurant. It was the first place that he and I first had a drink, but we never returned as I pushed to go to other locations in my search. When I mentioned to him as service was winding down on a Friday night that I was thinking of staying in one place, and that I was considering Martin's, a big toothy smile creeped slowly across his face, the gold caps on all four of his incisors shining in the florescent lights of the kitchen.

In all of our nights of going out to different places around the city, Mars pretty much let me decide where we went. At least I would suggest a part of town. He knew a place from that point. We went to multiple spots in Decatur, East Atlanta, Virginia Highlands, Edgewood, Midtown, Downtown, even Buford Highway, this long stretch of four lanes that ran towards the north of the city and was home to the majority of Hispanic and Asian residents of Atlanta. On at least three occasions Mars brought me to a restaurant or bar on Buford Highway where I was the only person in the place who couldn't read the menu. And while I felt uncomfortable as I entered each of those establishments, by the time we left that feeling had washed away. One night, after Mars and I finished three large, warm carafes of sake, he took me to a twenty-four hour Vietnamese joint where we picked up some sandwiches that we ate on the drive back. I'd never had a bahn mi before. The crusty sub roll stuffed with barbequed pork, cabbage, carrot, jalapenos, and this sweet mayo, was one of the best things I'd ever eaten.

Buford Highway began at Lenox Road at the southeastern corner of Buckhead. Mars refused to go to Buckhead. I went to a bar there once, a trendy place with "whiskey" in the name. There was a damn valet. I was so dumbfounded that I took the ticket and went inside. I was wearing jeans and a polo shirt. Immediately I felt like I didn't belong. The place was only about half full, but seemed like everyone in there had all come from the same benefit dinner. All I could see was obnoxious tailored shirts of varying color, most of them paisley, and fake tits bursting out of what must have been thousand-dollar dresses. I stayed for one drink which I sucked down quickly before finding the valet and getting back my car. On the drive back home I told myself first that there was no way Liberty would ever go into a place like that, and second, that it must be insane to live like any of those people. I'd interacted with rich people hundreds of times. For the most part they were easy to deal with. Just make them feel like they're the most important table in the restaurant and they'd probably buy a two hundred dollar or more bottle of wine and then hand you their black card at the end of the meal.

The most frustrating table I ever had was eight overtly wealthy narcissists. Individually, everyone at the table was pleasant and polite. The problem was that all eight of them interacted with me as though they were at a table for one. As if they couldn't hear any of the other people at the table also asking questions or placing orders. At this particular table, as I finished taking the wine order from an older man, the father to at least some of the other diners, another one of them asked if they could order a cocktail. I told the younger lady that the gentleman had just ordered both red and white for the table and I would be right back to get her order. She looked at me like I was an idiot and then resumed talking. Before I could take another step, the wife of the gentleman, who had to have heard him order wine from me, grabbed my arm and asked when she would be able to order an appetizer because she was starving. I pulled away rather easily and told her that I would send some bread to the table right away and would be back as soon as I grabbed the two bottles of wine that her husband had ordered and who was still staring at me with a look that wondered why I was still there. I returned with the wine and placed the red on the table and the white in an ice bucket. Trey had put down glasses for me. As I began to address the first woman who wanted to order a cocktail and had been staring at me since I re-approached, another woman from across the large round table waved her hand at me and asked why I hadn't taken a cocktail order or at least opened the wine. At this point I looked back at the gentleman who now had taken the bottle of chardonnay out of the ice bucket and was holding it out to me. I took the bottle from his hand and opened it as quickly as I could. The one thing that I always prided myself on was keeping my cool. I had never lost it at a table before. That streak was very close to coming to an end. I poured a taste of wine not bothering to wipe the lip of the bottle with a serviette. I looked at the old guy who had begun a conversation with the person to his left and was now ignoring me. At this point everyone else besides him was staring at me waiting to make their own demands. "Sir," I said, moving the glass a few inches closer to him. He looked back, annoyed, and then took a sip.

"I guess that's okay," he said turning away again. I began to put the bottle of white back in the ice so as to begin opening the red, but his wife's boney fingers wrapped around my forearm again. I looked over my shoulder and she was holding her glass out in front of my face. With as much composure as I could draw on from the depths of my experience I poured her wine.

"Go ahead. See if anyone else wants some. I don't understand why it takes so long to get a drink," she said to me and to the rest of the room as she used her salad fork to pull out pieces of ice from her water and plop them in the chardonnay. I began to offer wine to the younger woman who had first stopped me and she responded by ordering a Grey Goose martini, up, dirty, and with bleu cheese olives. I nodded, committing the drink to memory. I began to ask the man to her right if he would care for white wine and he cut me off and began to order appetizers for the table. I quickly put the bottle back in the ice and pulled out my notepad from my pocket as well as a pen. I wrote down the woman's cocktail first and then began to write down and repeat back to the guy the appetizers he ordered for the table.

"I'll have red," the woman next to him said to me before my pen stopped wiggling on the notepad. As I was opening the bottle of red, two other cocktail orders were barked at me, an old fashioned, and another Goose martini, this time with a twist. After the older man tasted the red and then said absolutely nothing at all, I poured a glass for the woman and then walked away from the table as fast as I could, ignoring another one of them that was trying to flag me down for something else. After thirty minutes everyone had a drink and appetizers were on the way. Had they let me just open the wine, then take a cocktail order, then appetizers, fifteen minutes wouldn't have been snatched from my life, and they would have been the happier for it. The rest of the meal continued in the same fashion. I couldn't even approach another one of my tables that was near them without being flagged down. It was the closest I'd ever come to walking out. But somehow I got through it. I dropped the check with gratuity included to the old man and then walked away praying to the restaurant gods that all of my effort would be worth it—that he'd leave me some extra on top of the tip. After they left I walked quickly over to the table and opened up the check presenter. Nope. Nothing extra written in on the tip line. The son-of-a-bitch didn't even bother to sign the thing at all. And he had walked off with my pen.

CHAPTER FIFTEEN

Over the years, I dealt with many wealthy people—most of whom were very nice and very generous—though always in the same environment: A restaurant. It was as though they appeared in all of their pomp and circumstance right outside of the front door and then vanished again in a puff of smoke. I always wondered what their lives were like. While I did have more than one encounter with a down to earth rich person, most of them seemed as though they lived by the same code. Like once they reached a certain number in their bank account, instructions were sent via golden carrier pigeon explaining how they must behave moving forward. First, the men must buy as many ridiculous dress shirts as possible, the top three buttons were left undone and the underside of each cuff was a strikingly different color. Sport coats were optional. Pants for men are suggested as bright red or salmon, but other hues are okay as long as the length is short enough to reveal their expensive loafers worn with no socks. The restrictions on women's attire are strictly age related. Over forty, Botox is a must—duck lips and a stretched expression. Also required regardless of age, is fake breasts, that must be shown off whenever possible. Brand names of course needed to be displayed while being perceived as mere happenstance. Certain actions must now be present as well. The men must refuse to hold their legs underneath a table when dining; instead they must cock their chair towards the aisle and sit cross-legged, impeding as many of the other patrons and staff as they can while pretending they have no idea that they are doing so. Both men and women must ignore their server at least half of the time they approach the table, in particular when they are attempting to place down silverware for the next course. When that occurs, the server must not only be ignored, but arms that are rested on the table must not be moved so that the silverware can be placed in the proper locations. Women must order multiple courses but under no circumstances are they to finish any of them. In addition, when more than two women are present at a table an unspoken competition over how little any of them can eat will occur. Lastly, both men and women regardless of age, must have strikingly bright white teeth. Teeth so stark white that anyone attempting to speak to them would be ever so slightly blinded and therefore at an inferior position—as they should be—unless already accustomed. I'd seen these actions repeated over and over and I'd always wondered if they extended back to their homes. Jim approached me after line-up one shift and presented me with the opportunity to find out for myself.

Chef had been asked to cook dinner for one of our most affluent regulars—one of the few who made the trip from Buckhead across town at least twice a month to eat his food. Jim asked me if I would be willing to accompany Trey and Thomas to serve the dinner at their house the following Tuesday. I accepted.

The house was massive. Two hundred yards of black asphalt snaked from the large metal gate on the edge of the street and led to three stories of dark red brick. The door from a large screened in porch opened to a short wooden dock that just stretched over the edge of a medium-sized lake. The driveway widened as Trey and I approached and he pulled over to the right side next to a retaining wall built of large stones. Thomas was already there and leaning on the side of his powder blue sedan. The three of us walked to the massive wooden double front doors. As we approached, the door on the left opened and a man in his late forties wearing a blue baseball cap stood behind. "Hey guys. You must be with the Chef," he said very quickly, his words running to together, before turning back around and walking into the house.

The three of us followed. The man introduced himself as Dennis, and told us that we could find the kitchen by following the hallway on the right, before disappearing into the massive house. The walls of the high-ceilinged entrance room were covered in art. The kind that its owners had bought on spec. At the advice of their buyer. Each piece was very different from the others, representing a variety of styles. Some I supposed could be considered avant garde, while others leaned towards more of a traditional form. But not a single one held any real emotion. Two winding staircases descended from the second floor. In between them was a grand piano on a raised platform. The place had smell to it. Nothing bad; it was like the fragrance of brand new shoes fresh out of the box mixed with mild potpourri was being pumped through the air vents.

"Come on, George," Trey said quietly, as he turned down the hallway Dennis had motioned towards. Pictures of family were hung on the wallpapered walls of the hallway that extended about twenty feet before opening up into a massive kitchen. Chef was standing before a giant black marble island placing small squares of crusty bread on a sheet tray. Two other men wearing white coats were also in the kitchen with their heads down working. I didn't recognize either one of them.

"Hey, guys," Chef said as he looked up from the sheet tray. "Thanks for making it."

"Yes, Chef," the three of us said in near unison. A woman in her mid-fifties entered the kitchen from a doorway on the opposite side of the room. Her hair was jet black and the plastic surgery on her stretched face gave her the appearance of constantly squinting.

"Hello, boys!" she said with fervor to the three of us as she walked in. She was wearing a pair of gray sweatpants and a purple t-shirt covered in sequins. It was odd seeing the combination of Botoxed lips and sweatpants. She was short, but walked with stride of a much larger person. Not that her legs were abnormally long; rather she held herself in a way that filled much more of the room than it should have. "I'm Marilyn," she said shaking each one of our hands. Thank you so much for coming to help. I'm really excited." Her voice was scratchy from what I assumed was years of smoking. "This is really going to be a fun night. The other five couples that we've invited just can't wait. Follow me and I'll show you where you'll be setting up." We followed her after a nod from Chef and ended up after a few twists just outside of a large dining room. "Over here," she said, pushing what looked to be a piece of the wall, but was actually a door leading to a small room with a counter top that ran along it's right side and a sink at the far end. Cabinets sat underneath drawers below the countertop, as well as above it, nestled against the ceiling. For whatever reason the ceiling in this room was at least five feet lower than both the hallway or the dining room. "You can put your things in here if you like. There's another door there to the left that goes directly to the dining room. You can use either one. I'm off to go and get ready, boys," she said spinning on her heel and walking quickly back in the direction we had just come. "Guests arrive at six," her voice bounced off of the walls as she rounded a corner.

Each of us had been holding a box since we arrived at the front door. We set them down on the counter. Mine was full of wine—the pairings for each course. Trey put down a split case of both sparkling and still bottled water, and Thomas placed his down last—a box containing hermitage wine glasses, designed to work best with wines from the Rhone valley in France. We found the other types of stemware needed in one of the cabinets above the counter. After getting the bearings of the small room and finding the two drawers of silverware we would need for dinner, we walked back to the kitchen to get together a game plan with Chef. "So the other guests are arriving at six," he said, now slicing a lobe of foie gras into inch thick pieces which he then quartered. "From what I gather, Marilyn wants to have a reception on the porch for the first forty-five minutes. Trey, why don't you man the bar—there's a fully stocked one out there—and the other two of you can pass hors d'oeuvres. It's four thirty now, so we've a got plenty of time to get everything set up to be as smooth as possible. Oh, yeah," he said looking up from his knife. "I forgot to introduce you. This is Jason; he's the chef at Riverview. He pointed to the shorter of the two men, but by far the widest. Not fat in any terms. He was stocky. His shoulders seemed at first glance to be almost half as wide as he was tall. "And this is Michael," he pointed again with his blade. He was skinny but looked as though he could hold himself up in a fight. He smiled genuinely and walked over and shook each of our hands while Jason had only nodded from across the other side of the island.

As if he knew we needed him, Dennis appeared silently. Thomas asked him if he would show us the way to the porch and he nodded enthusiastically before darting off back towards the the main entry room. He guided us through another series of hallways that turned at least four times before we reached a large room. A massive television hung on the far left wall in front of a large brown leather sofa and two lazy boys of the same material on either side. A pool table was to our immediate left. Outside of the pool table and TV and seating, everything else in the room was art. The same type that we first encountered when we entered the house. In this room, however, the "art", was almost a part of the room itself, rather than hung on walls or placed on a table. An over-sized wrought iron chair sat to the immediate right. Sitting in the chair was a rabbit made out of what looked like varying sized springs, or at least coils of red metal. In its mouth was an actual cigar. Behind the chair on the floor was a naked woman who appeared to be bathing in the floor itself. Her white ceramic upper torso and head with flowing wet hair disappeared into the black tiles of the floor only to have her bent knees reemerge. It was as though she was taking a bath in the floor. While the piece seemed as cold as the rest, it was by far the cleverest. At least a dozen other pieces sat in corners or hung from the ceiling. "Straight back," Dennis said pointing to another set of glass double doors trimmed in black wood. Then he was gone again.

What would be described as a sun porch by many people, although much larger than any I'd ever entered, was by far the homiest room I'd encountered yet. A full bar sat to the right. To the left were four cushioned chairs placed around a square glass table. In the center of the table was a small vase with white and yellow blossomed daffodils. The rustic wooden floor was covered almost completely with a simple tan rug. The kind that starts as a knot in the center and then spirals out in an oval. In the back right corner next to the glass door that lead to the short dock was a hammock.

The night itself was relatively simple: A reception out on the porch followed by four courses in the dining room and then dessert and drinks back out on the porch again. We agreed that Trey would stay behind and set up the bar while Thomas and I went to set up as much as possible for dinner itself. As we turned from Trey towards the main house the door to the porch opened and an older man stepped out. He was wearing ear buds and was completely immersed in whatever he was listening to. A joint hung out of his mouth—the scent of marijuana quickly dispersing. All of a sudden he noticed he wasn't alone. "Oh, hey," he said surprisingly calmly, pulling out one of his ear buds. "Just doing a little pre-gaming, you know. I'm Steve," he reached his right hand out to shake each of ours. "Good to see you again," he said when he shook Trey's. The hosts for the evening, I found out on the ride over with Trey, were his call party, meaning when they came in and he was working, they were sat in his section. Call parties were a win in our business. The guests themselves felt special having the same person take care of them each time they came in. And their experience was the better for it. The server came to know little details about what the guests liked or didn't like, ultimately providing a level of experience that could not occur with just a random server, regardless of how good they were. Steve wore expensive jeans and a gray and white dress shirt buttoned half way. His gray chest hair filled in the gap. He had a neatly trimmed beard and bright blue, blood shot eyes. "Care to partake," he said holding out the joint. "I won't tell," he said with a mischievous grin.

"No thanks," we each said in turn as he made eye contact.

"Okay then," he said putting the ear bud back in his ear and walking past us and out onto the dock.

The couples trickled in starting at about quarter of six. We had more than enough time to get set up and double check everything. Thomas already had two of each of the reds open and breathing and the whites on ice. I put together marking trays full of the silverware we would need for each course. The success of the night was not going to be because of execution. That was the easy part. What would make the night a hit was our ability to make people who already felt important to feel that much more so, while making the hosts—well at least Marilyn—feel a little more important than anyone else.

The cocktail reception with passed hors d'oeuvres went very smooth. Although Trey, who was the substitute bartender once a week, had brought with him two batched craft cocktails designed to pair well with the small bites, nearly every one there ordered a vodka and something. Be it soda, tonic, cranberry, or just on the rocks with a lime. There's some kind of strange relationship upper class people have with the stuff. I've seen it for years at my tables, but have never been able to put my finger on why vodka—excuse me—trendy vodka, was what they all wanted. My only thought is that because it is clear and tastes like pretty much nothing that some socialite years ago convinced themselves that it had fewer calories than say gin or whiskey. But that's not the case. They're all equal as long as the proof is the same. I guess it's one of those things we'll never know. At least not until the carrier pigeon comes calling.

Thomas and I passed the five hors d'oeuvres while Trey kept the vodka flowing. The foie gras that Chef had been cutting when we arrived had been seared and served simply on top of toast spread with a spiced apple jam. Wagu beef meatballs dipped in Korean barbecue sauce were skewered on long rectangular plates. Miniature crab cakes served with a sweet mustard sauce, a play on a Thai lettuce wrap using pulled pork instead of ground, and miniature grilled gruyere sandwiches cut into triangles were brought through the twisting hallways of the mansion and passed to the guests on the sun porch along with black cocktail napkins. Nearly all of the men gobbled up whatever was offered. The majority of the women took a few, but never more than one at a time, and refused the rest by politely saying that they were waiting and would try them later, which in rich lady talk means, "No, that will make me fat. I'm already feeling guilty from having one."

After more than a few suggestions from the three of us, the twelve of them finally made their way to the dining room and sat at two tables of six. Keeping custom, as there were more than five wealthy people at each table, they took at least five minutes to decide where to sit, discussing at length the importance of whom should be next to whom, and how that arrangement would influence the topics discussed. Once they finally sat down Thomas brought out the first wine.

The rest of dinner in the dining room was quite easy. Trey and I made sure that everyone felt attended to, and Thomas somehow never felt the urge to over explain the wine, or find a way to make anything more about himself than the people who were paying fifteen grand for dinner on a Tuesday. By the time the final savory course was cleared nearly everyone in the room was shit-faced. Not only had they enjoyed healthy pours of wine with each course, and usually a second helping, at least half of them had brought their various vodka concoctions with them. I have to say, not a single person said anything in a demeaning or rude tone. They asked for any and everything politely, but also with the confidence that there was no doubt at all that their requests would be fulfilled. They simply voiced their wants and those wants were met.

While dragging the party from the sun porch to dinner had been frustrating to say the least, convincing them to return, surprisingly was not. Maybe it was the promise of something sweet; maybe their intake of alcohol made them more amiable to suggestion; or maybe, just maybe, the entire shelf of needlessly expensive premium vodka above the bar on the large screened-in porch called to them in a way that no mortal outside of their social or financial standing could.

Dessert was a massive cheese platter—seven different kinds paired with preserves and nuts, as well as small, dense bites of flourless chocolate cake and chocolate icing served with a quenelle of vanilla ice cream. An extremely expensive bottle of Sauternes—Chateau d'Yquem 2005—was pulled out by one of the guests. Steve called me over to open the bottle. "This guy's a wine expert," he said, putting his arm around me. "He'll taste this and make sure it's good," he said to the guy who had produced the bottle. He looked at Steve and then at me with drunk confusion as I pulled my wine key from my pocket. Chateau d'Y'quem was regarded as one of the best Sauternes in the world. 2005 was the best vintage in over a decade. I shrugged my shoulders and smiled at the owner of the bottle trying my best to convey that I understood. He looked away, oblivious, but at least not pressing the issue. I scanned the room for Thomas. This was his kind of thing. Bumping up egos over wine. But he was nowhere to be found. I pulled myself free of Steve's arm and slid the blade of my wine key around the foil that capped the clear glass filled with golden liquid. I popped off the wrap of thin metal with a turn of my wrist and then eased my spiral corkscrew into the soft wood below. The cork free, I began to pour, but Steve pulled the bottle out of my hand spilling more than a splash of excellence on the floor without notice and then slid the glass I had put in front of him towards me. "You try it. You tell me if it's good, okay?"

"Yes, sir." I said, picking up the glass and then looking at the other guy now staring at me before I smelled deeply. "Wow," I said, putting on as much airs as I could. "This smells amazing. I see the vintage. Did you have trouble getting your hands on the '05? It's supposed to be the best in over twenty years." I embellished. If I lost any ground with this guy playing along with Steve's whims, I immediately regained it. And then some.

"It was for most," he said, a snarking smile jutting across his face. "But I have a guy. I got a case."

"Wow," I said, not in the least impressed, but doing my absolute best to appear as giving more than a shit. His attention quickly pulled him in another direction. I took this as an opportunity to slip back inside. I found Trey and Thomas in the small servant's room packing up the wine glasses and remaining bottles of water.

"George," Trey said to me curtly, but not abrasively. "I got the money. They gave us an extra two. Let's get the fuck out of here."

"Is Chef…"

"He's been gone for a half an hour. Told me we could take off as soon as they paid us."

"So we don't have to clean up or anything?"

"Chef said we can go. So we go. I'm sure they've got a staff of people coming in the morning—or shit, maybe waiting outside—to to come and clean this obnoxious place up." I didn't argue. Five minutes later Trey and I were on seventy-five south, an interstate that cuts through the middle of the city, heading back in the night. The absurdity of the evening still clinging to us both.

He dropped me off back at my place around ten-thirty. The Stroud's were out of town again and I been feeding the dogs for the past three days. For the most part they were used to me now. When I approached the gate, Licorice bounded up vigorously wagging his tail. Maude was calmly standing a few feet behind him. Harold didn't even bother to stand up. He was sitting only a few feet from his bowl looking at me.

When I first had to go into the backyard alone I had absolutely no idea how to do so without the possibility of Licorice getting out. He was always right there. He almost did on more than one occasion, but thankfully I was able to quickly close the gate behind me as I tried to keep him in with my body, resulting in success as well as more than a few scratches. Then I figured it out: Tennis balls. Licorice loved them.

He'd see me and run to the gate like always. And then I'd chuck one to the back of the yard. As soon as he took off, I'd slip right in.

I filled the bowls of food for each of them, made sure they had fresh water, and then began to walk back towards the gate. Harold and Maude began eating immediately, but Licorice was still in the back of the yard. Apparently he hadn't found the ball. I had a second one in my car. I could have just gone home. But I didn't. As I neared the gate, I heard a rush behind me. Licorice was sprinting towards me faster than I had ever seen him run, the yellowy-green fuzzy ball between his teeth. And he didn't stop. Maybe he wanted to. To give me the ball back so I could throw it again. But he didn't. I'm not really sure why, but I ducked. And thankfully so. Licorice took off about three feet in front of me and cleared not only my hunched back and my hands covering my head, but the fence as well. I stood up quickly and looked at him. He was more surprised than I was. I was certain that he was going to dart off and the rest of my night would be spent trying to corral him again. He turned his head away from me. "Licorice, sit!" I said firmly. Staring at him as though my gaze would be enough to hold him in place. He looked back at me. "Sit!" I said again with more bass in my voice than before. And he did. I opened the gate, walked over to him and held out my hand. He dropped the slobber-covered ball. And looked at me. I threw it back into the yard. "Go get it," I said with enthusiasm. He immediately darted back through the gate and I closed it as quickly as I could.

CHAPTER SIXTEEN

Maria was a middle and high school orchestra teacher. She only worked at the restaurant on Fridays and Saturdays, unless we were shorthanded, or someone begged her to cover their shift. She didn't talk about her other work much. Occasionally she would bring up a frustrating moment, but almost as soon as it left her mouth, she would change the subject as if she regretted saying anything at all. She did let slip to Jack early one Friday evening that she also played in a string quartet with a few other teachers in the county. They were having a concert after service at a local church that the viola player belonged to. Maria played the cello.

She was a solid server. Not a pro like Trey, but she understood the whole of it—she knew her deficiencies. Her service was slower than others, but elegant. She understood the moments during a meal that needed to be accentuated, and executed them as well as anyone I'd ever worked with. The other stuff she fell behind in. But she never complained and most of us around her had no problem filling in the gaps. Her smile was genuine. And her laugh. Since I began at the restaurant I can't recall a single complaint she was involved in. She both moved and spoke with a certain rhythm. Like her bow, drug delicately across vibrating strings.

I never went to church growing up. Although I had been in a number of them over the course of my life, I had never felt comfortable. Like just by being there something was expected of me. This time was no different. I sat with Trey and Mars on the right side of the aisle about three quarters of the way towards the back. Both of them wore a shirt and tie. Trey didn't surprise me at all. I wouldn't be surprised if he slept like that. But Mars was kind of a shock. I had never seen in him in anything but baggy t-shirts and jeans, or a hoodie during the winter. In fact, when I met the two of them out front as we planned the previous night, he looked me up and down, and shook his head at my jeans and green polo shirt.

Most of the people in attendance had been there for service. The place was pretty much full when the three of us sat down. After about five minutes the pastor stepped up and the large room fell silent. "We are very fortunate," he said, the tone of his voice still ripe with fervor, "to have the music of one of our own as well as the other very talented members of her string quartet played in the House of God." He was a relatively short man, but sturdy, with jet black hair that must have been dyed, as well as a groomed mustache of the same shade. His voice was deep and rich and he moved his hands dramatically when he spoke. Behind him on the stage were four chairs arranged in a trapezoid. After he stepped down and sat in the front row, Maria and three others walked out on to the stage. Their instruments were placed in front of each of the four wooden chairs: two violins, one viola, and Maria's cello.

Maria wore a dark green dress. Her red hair, always pulled up at work, hung past her porcelain shoulders. Two other women and a man filled out the rest of the ensemble. On the far left sat the guy—probably in his early thirties. He was a bit frumpy with thick rimmed glasses and bushy light brown hair that coiled out like fuzzy, erratic springs. To his right, the other violinist, was a short and squat woman, whose feet barely reached the floor. Her dark hair was pulled into a bun and the bright red dress she wore matched her lipstick. To her right, the viola player, was a willowy blond in a floral print dress who seemed as though she might blow away with a stiff breeze. And to her right was Maria.

After a minute or so to get situated and pick up their instruments they began to play. The first piece—I think it was Bach—was quite nice. Each of the four musicians took their turns carrying the methodical yet reverent melody as the piece progressed. I watched Maria as she played. Her hands which seemed so small to me at work when she cleared a table—sometimes my worry that she would drop something causing me to take an extra plate off of the table or out of her hands completely—were so resolute in the way she gripped the bow with her right, rocking back and forth, her subtlety swaying torso a counter balance, and with her left as she held down the strings on the long neck, her fingers moving with purpose and grace. They had memorized the piece so no music stands sat in front them. I could see Maria's face. As she played she held her head down, the left side of her chin tucked in. Although I was quite a ways away from the stage, I could still see that her eyes were open and she stared at the floor beneath her feet as though looking back in time, holding on to whatever memory clung to her as she played. I hadn't thought about playing music in so long. But as I watched Maria play the void that it had left in my life—in me—ached.

After the first piece ended and the audience applauded with Sunday fervor, the male violinist placed his instrument in front of him on the wooden stage and from behind his chair pulled out an acoustic guitar. They began to play again. I knew the melody after only a couple of measures; it was one of my favorites. It began in B minor. "Concierto de Aranjuez," was written by a Spanish composer, Joaquin Rodrigo, in the early twentieth century. I have always had a certain affection for minor keys. There's something about the steps between the notes—a shade off of those in the major that have been ingrained in our heads like love and war. The metered sadness of minor keys speaks to us all—to our humanity. Yet against the backdrop of our fallibility, on occasion, the minor turns major—for just a breath—like the first rays of sunshine breaking over the horizon. The sound of hope.

The last piece that was played was "All you need is love." The vocal melody was passed back and forth between the four instruments. It was a nice arrangement. Maria told the three of us out on the white front steps of the church that the last song they played had been a request by the pastor. We tried our best, each giving Maria an attempted guilt trip, to have her come out to eat. But she declined, explaining that she had already promised Maggie, the second violinist, that she would come to her house after the performance, along with the rest of the group and some of the other members of the church. She didn't seem too excited about going, subtly rolling her eyes as she turned to walk away after giving us each a hug. She smelled like lilies.

"Day drinking?" Mars said with a gleaming, puckish grin after she was out of sight. Trey glanced down at his watch. I figured it was about two o'clock.

"Where are we going?" Trey said as he looked up. I was shocked. I had invited Trey out multiple times and on each occasion he had politely declined, with a promised rain check that never seemed to come. I guess here it was.

"Martin's," I said quickly, thoughts of Liberty flooding my head. "The food's pretty good."

"Works for me," Mars said, spinning on his heels and heading towards his car.

"You know where it is?" I said to Trey.

"I think so."

Martin's was a brick building at the end of a small strip mall. The centerpiece of the tiny plaza was a mattress store that always seemed to be having some type of sale, although the prices never seemed to change. On the right of the mattress store was a laundromat advertising giant washers and dryers for large comforters, as well as laundry washed and folded for a certain cost per pound. That price seemed to change at least once a month. On the far side was an old school pharmacy that was owned by and only employed people who should have been retired. It sold rows of cheap candy underneath the checkout counter, and had a soda fountain in the back left corner where you could get an actual egg cream.

Six booths lined the aisle just inside the front door of Martin's. Behind the last booth on the right was a long bar that ended just outside of the kitchen. Across from the bar was a dining room. The walls of the place were forest green. The bar itself as well as the twelve wooden stools nestled up to it were stained dark brown. On either end, flat-screens showed whatever the best sporting event on at the time was. The walls were filled with large mirrors painted with logos of breweries as well as photos and framed posters of local sports teams. Mars and I usually sat at the end of the bar closest to the door, but this afternoon all of the seats were occupied. So the three of us sat in a wooden booth, the same color as the bar, just to the right of the glass front door.

It was one of the tables served by the bartender—an early thirties vanilla blond with a pony tail and large dimples. Mars ordered his usual. Trey and I split a pitcher of IPA. We ordered a few appetizers for the table and then sat in relative silence for the first ten minutes, waiting for the food to arrive, sipping our drinks. It was a pattern that Mars and I were accustomed to. And Trey was the quiet one. After the majority of the cheese fries, onion rings, and fried pickles were eaten, Mars ordered his third drink and Trey and I, our second pitcher. After a few more sips, Trey began to talk. I had never seen him utter more than ten words in a row before if it wasn't directly related to work. I had also never drank a pitcher and a half of high gravity beer with him either. "You know, I worked in a place like this just after I got out," he said after a long pull from his glass. "It was my first restaurant job, actually. I'd only been home for a few months and really wasn't sure what to do."

"Home from where? Prison?" Mars asked as he watched the television on the far side of the bar.

"The Marines."

"What did you do?"

"I'd rather not talk about it."

"Fair enough," Mars said, continuing to watch the screen.

"What were you saying?" I said, pulling the conversation back. Trey never talked about himself. I wanted to hear whatever it was he had to say.

"Oh. Yeah. So this place was kind of like this one. I started out waiting tables, and it was enough to get by and still put a little away for school."

"School?" Mars said. "What did you go to school for?"

"I didn't," Trey said flatly. "But at the time I wanted to be an engineer."

"Why didn't you?" Mars said back, again throwing off the story I was very curious to hear.

"I just didn't. Things came up."

"I hear that shit," Mars said, taking a large sip from his glass and then looking around for someone else who could bring him another.

"So this place…" I said.

"Yeah. So after about six months I started bartending at lunch. It was more work, but the money was better. And I got to take all of the tables before the night bartender came in after the last server was cut." He leaned back in the wooden booth and poured the rest of the pitcher into his glass. He took a sip, closed his eyes and then smiled, letting out a single chuckle. After a few seconds, he opened back his eyes and sat completely upright as he had before. He was my boy, but his posture was obnoxious.

"What's so funny?" Mars said, finally taking his eyes from the screen and looking at Trey.

"It's just—I haven't thought about this in years. But it's the same thing." He chuckled again. We both looked at him, curious. "So after the last server was cut, if people walked through the front door, I'd let them know that they could have a seat wherever they liked. For the most part, they sat at the bar, but a few times a week people would come in and sit down at a table. We had two dining rooms there. But the back one would be closed after the last server left. I laughed because I thought about this thing that would happen every once and a while. The servers were supposed to clean all of their tables before they left, but if they had some folks who just kept on sitting, they'd ask me if I'd clean it for them so they could go. It didn't happen very often so

I always said yes. Usually when people came in at three thirty for a late lunch, every table in the place had been wiped and set back up with roll-ups. But every so often one of those tables that sat forever would leave just before any others came in. And at least half the time when I told a small group of people to sit wherever they liked, on one of those days, where another table had just left, when I walked into the adjacent room to bring them menus, they would be sitting at that table—that one dirty table."

"But why?" Mars said, now fully pulled in.

"Control."

"What do you mean?"

"Well either the people chose to sit at the only dirty table in a room filled with clean ones because they thought it must be the best table, which is why it was the only one occupied before, and therefore they should sit there as well, because they deserve it—because by sitting at the best table they feel as though they are winning—that they are in control of their lives, or because they simply—maybe subconsciously, maybe not—they want to sit there so that I have to awkwardly clean it while they thank me in the same tone that they would their butler, which of course they don't and never will have. Control."

"Damn. That's some twisted shit," Mars said, disengaging and trying to flag down the bartender, for another drink.

"It's the same stuff that we deal with all the time," I said.

"Yup," Trey said.

"Keep my ass in the kitchen," Mars replied. "Y'all can keep that Dr. Phil shit to yo'selves."

We sat in relative silence for the next hour or so, Trey quiet again, and Mars on his phone either playing a game or having an extremely engaging text conversation. I watched the television in the reflection of the window in front of me. A baseball game. I couldn't help but smile every time someone got a hit, or walked, and then ran to third base.

We stopped in downtown Decatur after we left Martin's—this divey place that had been there since before the area was trending, so that Mars could flirt with the bartender. This pink haired chick with more tattoos than he had. Trey shot pool with an older guy who looked like Jack Nicholson and I sat at the end of the bar and watched the door. Waiting.

Time slipped away, like memory, as it tends to when muddled with drink, and the three of us ended up at this all-night diner on Cheshire Bridge Road just barely over the official city limits of Atlanta. Only a few of the booths that hugged the windowed right side had occupants. We chose one towards the back of the place. A woman in her mid-twenties walked slowly over to the table after a few minutes. She was prettier at a second glance than I initially thought when I walked in and saw her talking on the phone behind the long counter opposite the booths. She was thin, with dark brown hair tied in a loose ponytail and light freckles that showed underneath the foundation on her face. "Hey, guys," she said quickly, as though she had had too much coffee. "Something to drink?" Mars and I ordered waters and Trey a diet coke. "Be right back," she said walking away. The three of us looked over the thick, laminated spiral bound menus in silence until she returned. She put the drinks down and then pulled a tattered pad and pen out of her short maroon apron. She smiled nervously and wiped her nose quickly with her left hand as she held the pad and pen in her right. While she couldn't have been more than twenty five, her eyes held a weight to them that I had only seen in people at least ten years older. A sadness. She rocked back and forth waiting for one of us to speak. Mars ordered a patty melt. Trey, a three egg omelet with sausage, peppers, and onions as well as a side of hash browns. As she wrote down Trey's order, the sleeve of her stained white dress shirt fell down her left forearm. Six horizontal scars beginning about four inches behind her thumb were a pale white against the more evident freckles not covered up by makeup. She looked at me, expecting an order and saw where my eyes fell. She quickly pulled the sleeve up to her wrist and then held her arms low so that both of them remained covered.

"I'll have a BLT," I said quickly darting my eyes somewhere else. "On rye. With fries."

"Got it." She walked away, looking back once more towards the table as she wiped her nose again with the back of her hand. She spoke with a hesitance, a subtle vibrato to the timbre of her words, as though she expected something terrible to happen. She was like a wilted flower—her petals once vibrant and firm, now drooping and beginning to brown. But only subtly and at the very edges.

CHAPTER SEVENTEEN

One Saturday night in late March, the soup was French onion and Chef was in a foul mood. The average Saturday night is a bear. On occasion, you have an easy one where all of a sudden the night is winding down and you don't feel as though you want to strangle someone. Bad Saturdays are like Beethoven's 7th Symphony, second movement: the Allegretto.

That night started out with a subtle pulse of strings. I was both intrigued to find out why the soup was the dreaded French onion, but also wary. Saturday was hard enough without anything extra to pile on your shoulders. As the first few tables trickled in, I chatted with Trey, Maria, and Thomas in the server station, which meant that Trey didn't say a thing and I interjected occasionally as Thomas went on in an attempt to impress Maria. To say that it was obvious he had a crush on her would be an understatement. But she was kind. And while she kept him at arm's length, she did so in a manner that didn't make him feel as though he had completely lost. She really did have a beautiful smile.

As I greeted my first table the pulse of strings had been given to another in a higher register and the original ones began a different melody—another layer—as the volume of the night began slowly to rise. The goal on a Saturday night is to get my first table up and out of my section as fast as possible. I wasn't concerned about the tip. Having one table crossed off my list before the crescendo of the night occurred is much more valuable. And in that regard I was screwed.

The table of four was made up of two couples in their late forties. Each couple had brought their own bottle of wine, which was fine with me, but when they instructed me to decant only one of the cabernets once I had brought them their cocktails, I knew that they weren't going anywhere any time soon. I accepted it and moved on. Five minutes later I was sat again with a deuce. I greeted them quickly. It was two guys—academics my best guess—one older and one younger, who were anything but warm with me when I said hello, but seemed content to keep their bubble around them. Not needy at all.

I looped through the kitchen to see if any food needed to be run. On busy nights there are stretches where running food, while it is part of my job, is nearly impossible. To compensate for this, I try to carry as many plates out of the kitchen before I get busy as I can. Chef, who usually spoke with an evenness, especially before the chaos settled in, barked at me when he saw me enter the kitchen to take two appetizers—a Hamachi poke and grilled quail with kumquats—to table fifty-two to share. "Yes, Chef. Fifty-two. Share," I responded quickly as I picked up the dishes with black linens that had been folded into hand sized rectangles so as not to leave fingerprints.

As I was given my third table of the night, the melody, still rising in volume, was passed again amongst the strings; what was only a pulse earlier had now become more aggressive and began to compete with the other sounds of the night. I had still yet to get an order from

ONE DIRTY TABLE

my first table, which was going to turn into a problem shortly, but my second table, although having sent me away twice already, told me what they wanted when I returned the third time. Two glasses of wine and entrées. I told them that it would be a little while before their food arrived, but they said it wasn't an issue as long as there was bread. The third table was another table of four. A family. The father who appeared to be in his late sixties asked for the wine list before I could get a word out of my mouth after I approached them. I had no problem with that, giving them a quick spiel and then leaving him time to look over the list.

I realized then, in that moment, that the tables who were in the majority—those full of decent people who were here for a special moment of their own—allowed me to deal with the others: the few that dominated my time and emotion. The good ones kept me from losing it all. And most of the time, I never gave them a second thought. I was consumed by the negative. While I should have been talking to my peers about the tables I had that were full of kind, decent, people, instead I kept my focus on the ones who made me work harder than I should have. The irony being that the table of four—a family celebrating the birthday of the mother at the table—people who enjoyed every moment of their experience—those were the ones that I could leverage so that the others—ones consumed by attention and arrogance—could be taken care of without major issue. In a perfect world, those guests that comprise the majority, yet are forced to be the least of my priority, would surpass every douche and asshole who needed to feel important. It's a damn shame.

I walked quickly back over to the first table who was engrossed in conversation. I waited patiently for almost a minute before I interrupted. "Are there any questions?" I asked quietly but with tempo, having waited until one of the guys who had been talking took the last sip of his old fashioned. The four of them looked at me like I was speaking in tongues. I just stared back, a smile pulled tight at the corners of my mouth.

"Um. I don't have any questions," one of the women said to the other three at the table, not to me. She was wearing a red dress that matched perfectly her earrings, her nails, and the small purse that sat on the table to the right of her vodka soda. The other guests didn't respond, instead picking up their menus for what was probably the first time. "But maybe we can order an appetizer," she said again to the table.

Before anyone else had a chance to respond I interjected. "I'll give you another couple of minutes before I come back and take your whole order. May I pour wine for the table?" I said with more weight to my words than when I had arrived. The other guy, the one who hadn't been talking incessantly about his business trip to Paris, looked directly at me and nodded. I picked up the glass container and then poured wine for all four of them with a touch of pomp and circumstance to linger a little longer and keep them focused on the menus. "I'll be right back," I said as I placed the decanter back on the round, metal coaster in the middle of the table.

I looked back at the two academics, one of whom had pulled out a tablet and was showing something to the other as he shoved a piece of buttered bread in his mouth. They didn't need me. Perfect. I walked past the last table that I had been given. The father was still looking at the wine list. I thought about approaching them to move the process along or at least offer for Jim to come back and talk wine, but after one step, Thomas walked quickly past me with plates in his hands, made intentional eye contact and said, "hands." I pivoted and walked straight to the kitchen.

Chef Raymond was angrier than I had ever seen him. "I don't understand!" he said with venom. The strings still swelling in their layered melodies. "Jim! Where's Jim?" he said looking back towards where I stood. "Someone get me Jim!" I backed away into the server station and then walked as quickly as I could without breaking into a run. I scanned the dining room before heading to the front of the restaurant. Jim was looking over the shoulder of the hostess, a rectangular brunette with stylish glasses named Catherine.

"Jim," I said interrupting. He looked back at me in confusion before the look on my face told him of the necessity of my words. "Chef needs you right away. He's not happy." He looked at me again as he took off in long strides back towards the kitchen. "I'm not sure what happened," I said as I accelerated right behind him. Abruptly, he said, "passing," and the two of us stopped walking and hugged the wall to our right with our backs as an elderly couple walked past. As soon as they were clear of where he was standing, he took off again. I didn't follow. I still had to get an order from my first table and check in on the guy with the wine list at my last. He was still looking at the list and his wife was engaged in conversation with the older of the two children, a young woman in her mid-twenties. The son was on his phone. I walked quickly over to the two couples and pulled out a pen. After a couple of questions I got their order in whole—three courses—salads, apps, and entrées. Food had just been placed down on my table of two. The guy with the wine list had finally put it down. If I checked on the two-top and then quickly rang in the order I had just received, I could get back to talk wine before it was apparent that I was missing.

I turned right towards the computer terminal that was in a small nook just inside the dining room. Jim sped past me with plates in his hand before I could get five feet. "Hands, George," he said firmly, making eye contact as he rushed by. Had he only said "hands,"

I would have kept going and rung in my order. But the addition of my name meant that at this moment I didn't have a choice. I darted into the kitchen and pulled out the black linens that I kept tucked in my back left pocket. My foot tapped the floor anxiously in rhythm to strings that had now begun to drown out the rest of the noise around me. The sounds were still there. I could still hear them. But I had to strain. I quickly grabbed the two bowls of soup—French onion—at Chef's barking order and rushed out of the kitchen. Beads of sweat had formed on my forehead.

 I stepped out of the curtain that led to the dining room and nearly spilled both bowls of soup on Catherine who was standing just outside. I stopped inches from her, the liquid rising to the far edge of the bowls before settling back down without spilling a drop. "You have three at table forty-one," she said with a plastic smile. At that moment the wind section and percussion took over the first melody while the strings, now at their apex, took over the second. Everything else beyond the raging torrent in A minor was drowned out. I now had to take the soup in my hands to the table on the other side of the dining room, greet the table that had just been sat, touch base with the father which could also mean getting stuck taking an order as well, and I had still not put in the order for my first table. I had to create a plan, prioritizing everything in the absolute correct order, or I was screwed. I took off with the bowls in my hands. I passed Thomas whose eyes were filled with panic. No help there. Then I saw Trey began to turn away from one of his tables. I stopped for five seconds and waited for him to see me. He made eye contact and walked quickly over. "Go to thirty-three and take a wine order if you can," I said, not hearing a word that left my mouth before turning away towards the destination of the soup. He didn't say a thing, only stepped with purpose towards my table.

As I hurried back towards my section he was pointing out a bottle in the open list and said something that made the guy laugh. One down. The music still pounded. I saw one of the server assistants, Jose, a good kid who worked hard. "Jose," I mouthed, hoping that somehow the vibrations reached his ears, "Take bread to twenty four. And bring, olive oil, vinegar, and butter. Please." He looked at me funny for a moment, nodded, and then rushed off.

I went over to the nook with the computer and grabbed three menus. I wiped my forehead with the linen I keep in my other back pocket for just that reason, and went to my newest table. It was three men in suits. Expensive suits. Surprisingly they were quite attentive when I approached them and engaged me when I went over the menu. Lawyers. I saw Jose drop off the basket of bread as well as the other accoutrement that I had requested. I asked if any of the guys would care for something to drink and two of them mouthed an order for expensive bourbon on a large ice cube and the third a peaty scotch, neat. I met Trey on the way back to the computer, who handed me a torn piece of paper from the small notebook he took orders on. "Bottle of Mersault, I'm grabbing it; there's the order," I read from his lips.

I nodded. I quickly rang in the order of my first table, triple checking it before sending it to the kitchen. Then I rang in the drinks for the three guys. Underneath the small counter where the computer was in the corner nook was a cabinet where glassware was stored. By this time of night it was usually bare, but I was in luck as I opened it and found four Burgundy stems already polished. Holding the glassware upside down in my left hand behind my back, I walked over to the two couples and told them that their first course would be out shortly and that bread was on the way. I filled all four of their glasses with my right hand, but only half way, leaving enough in the decanter so as to avoid having to be asked to decant the second bottle, and then walked away towards the family. As I finished placing down the wine glasses, Trey appeared and handed me the bottle of white wine. I poured the father a taste. He smiled warmly and nodded. I filled the rest of the glasses and then walked back to ring in their order. Slowly, as I walked through the dining room, other sounds began to creep back to my ears as the pounding melody began to fade and was replaced by an almost soothing one led by gentle strings and woodwinds, both alternating in falling scales. The apex of my night was over. I didn't fall. There would be more to come, but at this point, my section was full and everyone was satisfied.

 I rang in the order for the family and then picked up the drinks for the three suits from the bar. When I dropped them off, it was obvious they wanted to chat and sip. I went back to the kitchen to see if I could run any food and saw that my first course on the couples' table had just been sold. With nothing to run at the moment, I circled back to the server station and out to the dining room to find Trey and see if I could repay him for saving my ass. As it turned out I could. He had just gotten two tables in less than five minutes and sent me to one of his other tables to clear it, mark it with silverware, and fire the next course. After firing the food I noticed that I needed to do the same on the couples' table as well as clearing entrées and dropping dessert menus on the deuce.

 The original melody now returned, but at a quicker and lighter pace and now in A major. I still hustled around the dining room, still having to stop to wipe my brow, but I had found a rhythm. I took the order from the three guys after checking on the first course at the family table. As I turned away from them, I noticed that the talkative man at the couples table was pouring out the rest of the decanter into his own glass, leaving the other three glasses with barely two or three sips. The academics declined dessert, asking only for their check. As

I walked away I could see the woman in red drain her glass and then look around for me. I quickly printed the check and dropped it off before abruptly walking over to my first table. "Would you like me to decant your other bottle," I said to the woman in red.

"Yes. Yes, that would be good," she replied, motioning to her husband to hand me the bottle of wine from the brown leather cylindrical case that sat on the ground in between the two of them. I took the empty decanter away along with the bottle and picked up the check from the two-top. I swiped the credit card and brought back the check to the two gentlemen. After pouring the wine into the bulbous glass container in the server station, I placed the decanter as well as the empty bottle and cork on a rectangular tray. As I stepped out of the curtains into the dining room, Thomas, looking to his right and not in the direction he was moving, clipped my left elbow. The tray in my left hand wobbled and along with it, the decanter than sat on it. It was like a scene from The Matrix. Everything slowed down nearly to a stop as I tried to regain the balance of the tray while watching the glass lean towards the floor. If it fell, I would be so behind I don't know if I could have caught up. But just as the decanter began to tip, I caught it with my right hand. The empty bottle fell over on the tray, but not off of it. My heart pounded and I steadied myself and the tray before taking a deep breath. A second late reaching out to grab the decanter of wine, an inch off, and my night would have been ruined. One second. One inch.

Over the next thirty minutes, I was sat with another deuce at the same table as before, both of my four-tops were eating their entrées, and the three suits were on their second round waiting for their first course. The melody continued at the same pace, more hopeful than in the beginning of the night. Then another thirty minutes later as the couples' table was looking over dessert menus and the family of four needed their entrées to be cleared, the three guys were waiting for their main course, while my newest table waited for their salads, the music swelled again, this time much more abruptly than before, but pounded just as hard. Thirty seconds earlier Catherine had stopped me as I tried to walk into the server station. "You have six at table sixty." I looked back at her in disbelief. "Jim said for you to take it," she said with that counterfeit grin.

And again all other sound faded to nothingness as the melody raged and crashed around me. I went immediately to the new table on the other side of the dining room. Fortunately, the six of them—another set of couples, but in their sixties, had brought drinks with them from the bar. And they were all nearly full. I said hello briefly, placed down menus and the wine list, and found out what type of water they preferred. I had at least ten minutes before I would need to get back. As I walked over to check on the entrées that had just landed on the three-top, I saw Jose clearing the family table. The newest two-top was still waiting for their first course, but they were engaged with each other. I covered the short amount of ground over to my first table, which should have been gone already, and took their dessert order. Along with two desserts for the table, the guys ordered double espressos, and the woman in red, hot tea. Damnit! Hot tea took forever. I rushed back to the server station, got the loose leaf chamomile tea steeping in a mesh cup that sat in the mouth of a black iron pot, and set the small digital timer for five minutes. I dropped off dessert menus for the family of four and saw that the first course was on the two top. I wanted to ring in dessert, but if for some reason Jim ran the sweets to my table and one of them asked about a drink that wasn't there before hand, it would be my ass.

There is no worse time as a server to get a new table than when one of the tables in your section is on dessert. While it might seem tame, the steps of service for dessert is surprisingly difficult when coupled with other variables. The timing has to be just right. Coffee, tea, port, scotch, and god forbid coffee drinks all must be timed so that they arrive piping hot or perfectly chilled and not too far in advance of the desserts themselves. I went back to the server station to check on the tea and then went to the computer to ring in their desserts, a toffee pudding and a panna cotta. Before I ducked back in the server station I glanced in the direction of the six-top. It was on a raised level of the dining room so I couldn't see all of the faces, but the two that I could see told me that I still had a few minutes.

I set up my tray for beverage service with a cup and spoon for the tea, the pot itself, as well as a matching iron coaster that the pot would sit on. I pulled the first double espresso and set it down next to the empty coffee up. As I began to make the second, Jim came in through the curtains. "What can I do for you?" he said directly to me. Whenever I was asked by a boss if I needed anything, my first instinct was to decline as a point of pride. But having managed a floor before, I also knew that everyone needed help occasionally and I had always been willing. Jim was the same way, but I still liked being the one person he didn't have to worry about after spending so much time myself worrying about a whole dining room.

"The espressos are for one and four on thirty-two, the tea, seat three. And I need a dessert mark,"

"Heard," he said, although I could only read his lips, picking up the tray as I set down the second espresso. I followed him past the curtain and went to the family of four.

"I don't think we'll be having dessert," the father said to me, having collected the four menus and handing them to me as he spoke. "I wish we could, but we're all so full. And we have a cake waiting at home. Everything was great by the way. Especially you. The service was just great." I thanked him and brought the check right back. He handed me a card after quickly looking over the receipt and I swiped it and brought it promptly back to the table. I looked at the other two tables near me. The table of two had just been cleared and needed to be set for entrées and the suits were still finishing theirs. Luckily their drinking pace has slowed down and they still had half full glasses. I brought out the mark for the two-top and then began to walk towards the table of six.

The melody that had consumed everything again, gracefully transitioned into another, quieter sweeping passage. Simple and warm. Allowing the rest of the sounds of the restaurant to coexist. The table of six was ready to order and didn't seem at all as though they were perturbed for having to wait. Each of them ordered another of the same cocktail they arrived at the table with, salads, and then main courses. Two of the women ordered appetizers for their entrees. I placed the order for the drinks first and then food. As I left the table of six after checking on their first course which had just dropped, my first table of the night having finally paid, the suits having a final round along with their check which had been paid as well, and the deuce happily enjoying their main course, the initial melody returned. But this time it was just barely there, just beneath the surface, before swelling for just a measure, and then fading away for good. While I still had two tables and shutting down the restaurant to look forward to, Maestro Beethoven had put down his baton.

CHAPTER EIGHTEEN

By the beginning of our senior year, Arthur had become a crashing wave. He was regarded as one of the best high school quarterbacks in the state. And Liberty was still by his side. Yet for the past two years, once or twice a month, I would find a folded piece of paper in my locker asking me to meet up. We only talked. I was her nostalgia. It allowed her to keep up the airs as Arthur's girl—the most popular in school—but still remember who she was. In a way I was a drug. And over the two years her desperation, although subtle, to remember who she used to be—who she still wanted to be—grew. And with that, our sporadic yet eventual meetings became more and more intense.

While I thought I knew what it was to be in love years earlier, I learned otherwise over the two years that passed. What I had come to feel for Liberty now completely overwhelmed those innocent and fragile feelings I held onto years before. But while I yearned for her, I never made a move. On the surface Arthur and I were still friends, but the depth of understanding we once shared had shallowed considerably. But something of what it once was still lingered in the current. Occasionally we would actually have a real conversation. Even though he was wrapped in himself, I knew that the Arthur that I remembered was still there, somewhere beneath it all.

I hadn't met up with Liberty for almost two months when I found another note. It had been the longest gap since that first piece of folded paper Sophomore year. I had spoken to her more than once, but it didn't mean anything. While I could tell that Arthur also knew that our friendship had changed over the years, I don't think for a second that he thought it was as frayed as I did. He still occasionally came over for dinner. At least twice a month he and I would go and shoot baskets on the blacktop behind our old elementary school. The rims were about six inches lower than they should have been. Arthur could dunk a regulation goal. I could just get it over the rim at the goal in the far right, back corner of the three side by side courts. Liberty usually came. And she and I would talk. But it wasn't real. It was me pretending to like talking to the other her. The one that I knew she hated being, but did so for him. At least she told herself that. She never played with us. Instead she sat on the grassy hill that led down from the school and wrote in her green notebook. That was the one thing that she hadn't let go of as her popularity skyrocketed. She looked and acted like a different person. But she still had poetry. I asked Arthur once if she ever let him read any of her stuff. "Of course she would," he responded, letting me know he hadn't read a word. Sometimes it felt like he just couldn't see people for who they were; he only had the capacity to see them as he wanted them to be. Maybe that was why he owned the moment. The confidence had to always be there. Not just when the moment called for it. If he started to question the people around him—had any doubt that they questioned him—the moment would suffer.

She let me read what she wrote. Not every time, or any page that I turned to in her notebook. She would pick out the poem and then sit and watch as I read. She would hold the fingers of her right hand close to her mouth, but never letting herself bite down on one of her colorful nails. Most of what Liberty wrote held the same amount of sadness as her green eyes. It wasn't overwhelming. But it was there. That's the thing about eyes. You can train the muscles in your face to behave a certain way, make the words coming out of your mouth say things you don't believe. But no matter how good you are—even if you've convinced yourself that your life is exactly as it should be— your eyes will betray you. Yet while that layer of sadness touched her words, it did so, as with her eyes, with depth and beauty. The last time we were together she let me read a poem she had written recently. It was untitled:

I would that I were a leaf upon a felled tree pushed over by the wind and the rain; that I would lay upon the forest floor green, and full of life.

Although my journey down would be more abrupt and savage,

I would have fallen with purpose, pulled down with the rest, cushioning the blow.

I would lay upon the forest floor with those who have fallen before me— of their own choice or not— listening to their wisdom crackle beneath the soles of strangers.

Maybe before my veins begin to harden and I begin to slowly fade, we could all, as one, be righted— our roots again firmly entrenched in our past— those who have come before and have been ground to dust and now hold us up with their humility.

I met her after school at the same park that we had gone to after the first time she put a note in my locker. And like before she was sitting on the swings. She was wearing a green sweater. The sleeves were long and hid her small hands beneath the cuffs. The outlines of her fingers grasped the segmented metal links that connected the black rubber seat to the horizontal pole above. In her ears were large, silver hoop earrings. I sat in the black rubber seat next to her. She smiled with her mouth but not her eyes before she looked away and let silence wash over us both. I rocked back and forth, my feet dragging in the broken wood chips beneath me for at least two minutes before she said a word.

"I think he's cheating on me."

"What?" I said, after taking a moment to digest.

"Arthur—there's this junior… Melissa Perkins." She sat perfectly still in the swing now—a calmness taking over as she spoke. As much as I had many problems with who Arthur had become, I didn't think he would do something like this to Liberty.

"Are you sure?"

"Someone saw them."

"Who?"

"Becky Slater. She told me on Tuesday that she had seen Arthur drop Melissa off at the end of her block twice in the last week, right in front of Becky's house. Melissa lives almost at the other end of their street." She let her feet dangle from the swing and swayed slowly.

"What are you going to do?"

"I'm not sure. You didn't know, did you?" she said, turning her head towards me, her glazed eyes burning.

"No." I snapped back, meeting her stare. She held my gaze, searching, and then dropped her head.

"I'm sorry."

"It's okay." I filled with rage. I know that Liberty and I didn't tell Arthur about our meetings, but all we did was talk. Although I wanted her more in a way that I hadn't wanted anything else, we were only friends. And he had her. He had always had her. While I had been forced to watch with a front row seat. And he's cheating on her. What an asshole! Then the anger began to subside and my thoughts began to push through my emotions. Anger then was replaced with hope. Maybe this is exactly what was supposed to happen. But then just as abruptly as that thought had filled my mind, guilt pushed it out and then remained in its place. This is not the way things were supposed to happen. This is not how I wanted to have my chance.

"There's a party tonight after the game. It's at Thompkins park. Are you gonna go?" she said, now leaning back in the swing and staring up at the sky, her back level with the ground and calmness again wrapping itself around her. A dangerous calmness.

"I'm not sure. Are you going to talk to Arthur?"

"I don't know. I'm not really sure what I'm going to do."

We sat in silence. I wanted to say so much. To tell her how I felt. To tell her how I would never have cheated. To tell her that I'm here. I'm here right now. That she didn't need him. But I didn't say a thing.

"Thanks," she said, breaking the silence.

"Yeah," I said back. "Sure thing." I couldn't believe that was my response. Maybe anything with a touch of emotion would have led to everything else that I wanted to say, but couldn't. After another bout of silent rocking, Liberty got out of the swing and began to walk to her car. I followed.

"I've got to get to the game," she said as she turned the key in the driver's side door. "Are you going?"

"No."

"Well, you should come to that party tonight, George," she said turning her head towards me as she opened the door. She smiled before getting into the car. A cold smile.

"I'll try," I said as she closed the door and cranked the engine. I stood there in the road and watched her drive away.

Around ten o'clock, when the light in my parents' bedroom went dark, I climbed quietly down the stairs in my socks and eased open the front door. Our driveway had just the smallest degree of slope, but it was just enough that I could take off the parking brake of my mother's car and roll into the street.

The parking lot adjacent to Thompkins park was nearly half full when I pulled into a space just inside the driveway, as far away from the rest of the cars as possible. Regular people drove like assholes; drunk teenagers made them seem like saints. I wasn't going to take a chance at having to explain to my father as to where a mysterious dent came from. The park was good sized—about a football field—and the pavilion where at least two kegs of beer would be hidden in trash cans was in the back right corner, nestled up to the cemetery. Trees, mostly white oak, with scattered maples and dogwoods surrounded me as I walked. I could hear the party before the pavilion opened up in front of me. The local police knew exactly what was happening. But they also knew that Arthur would be here. No one was going to do anything to harm the pride of Pensdale. That would be the same as harming Pensdale herself. So the parties here were never busted. But if you weren't Arthur, driving home was a different game.

"George!" Arthur called at me from one of the picnic tables next to the pavilion. "What's up, homie!" he said with vigor as I approached, before walking quickly over to me and punching me in the shoulder. "You haven't been to one of these in forever. Did you see the game?

Can you believe it?" he said quickly before turning away and walking back into the throng. "Wooo!" he cried out, chugging the remainder of the beer in the red plastic cup in his hand. I walked over to one of the trash cans and poured myself a beer. The mass of partiers—at least fifty students—formed a loose circle of clumps around the pavilion. I weaved my way through the raucous bodies, looking for Liberty. She was nowhere to be found.

Everyone was talking about the game. Apparently they were down by three touchdowns at the end of the third quarter. But then Arthur mounted a comeback. As the clock wound down he threw a ball from midfield that was intercepted. It should have been the end of the game. But instead of just falling to the ground, the cornerback who picked off the ball tried to run it back. Arthur hit him so hard that the ball popped free. It was scooped up by the tight end, who quickly tossed the ball back to Arthur who broke three tackles before diving into the end zone. An extra point would have tied the game, but Arthur took the snap from the two-yard line and threw a strike to the back of the end zone for the win.

After walking the perimeter of the party twice looking for Liberty, I filled my cup for a second time and sat down, my back leaning against the trunk of a large oak about fifty feet away from all of the action. I sat there sipping my beer and wondering why I had come here in the first place. After a few minutes, loud cheering from behind me caught my attention. There she was. There was Liberty. Standing on the wall that separated the park from the cemetery. I jogged over to the sporadic clumps of students that had now amalgamated into a solid mass. Watching Liberty swaying back and forth on the wall clutching a bottle filled with brown liquor by the neck.

She threw the bottle. It shattered on the corner of the closest picnic table. Arthur was in the front of the crowd. "I…have…something to say," she said, her feet on the green moss that crept over the wall. "I—" she took a step towards Arthur, but the moss beneath gave way. Liberty fell. It all happened in slow motion. At first it seemed as though she was going to slip backwards into the cemetery, but at the last moment one of her feet found traction again and propelled her into the park. Right into Arthur's outstretched arms.

I didn't realize while I was doing it, but I had moved from the back of the crowd to the front, and now stood only a few feet away from Arthur and Liberty. She turned her head towards me, cradled in his arms. Whatever words she had planned on saying were gone now. The look in her eyes was somewhere in between shock and confusion. A haze had washed over her and replaced vitriol with first fear and then relief so quickly that they both still lingered at the same time. She turned her head away from me as Arthur put her back down on her feet slowly. Her hands held onto his shirt with white knuckles. "Everything is okay, baby," he said to her as he used his right hand to brush her hair from her face. She didn't respond. Then Arthur saw me. "George. George," he said. "Come here for a sec. Look, can you take Liberty home? I mean not right home. She's shit-faced. But can you take care of her?" I stared back at him. Into his eyes. "You're the only one I trust, okay?" he said to me, looking back at her with affection. "Please?"

"Okay. But it doesn't really look like she wants to go."

"I'm pretty sure she's about to pass out," he said, easily pulling off her left hand from his shirt, her grip severely slackened.

"Okay. Here," I said, wrapping my right arm around her and steadying her.

"I'll see you later, baby. Just go with George," he whispered into her ear as he let go of her completely. She looked up at me. Her eyes now glassier than before. We walked slowly through the trees back to my car. As we reached the edge of the parking lot, my car still on the far side, she stopped abruptly and threw up all over my shoes. She mumbled apologies as I carried her across the black asphalt. As we pulled out onto the street she could barely keep her eyes open. A minute later she was asleep. I couldn't take her home like this, so I drove. I got onto the interstate and headed north for about forty-five minutes, before turning around. My hope was that she'd get enough sleep to be able to go back home. She slept the entire time.

I nudged her awake as I pulled onto the curb in front of her house. "Arthur?" she said groggily as she opened her eyes.

"It's George," I said. "You got really drunk and Arthur wanted me to take you home since I hadn't drank too much." I added the last part.

"Okay," she said, closing her eyes again. I nudged her again.

"Liberty. Liberty," she looked at me again like a cat abruptly woken. "You've got to wake up." I opened my door and walked around to her side of the car. I opened the door, nudged her awake once more and then pulled her to her feet.

"Is Arthur coming?" she said, still dazed, but much more awake.

"I don't think so. I'm sure you'll see him tomorrow. You really need to get into bed. Come on." As we reached the front door, all of the lights in the house were still off. Liberty pulled her keys out of her purse and handed them to me. "Are you okay to make it to your room?" I said after opening the door.

"Yeah. I think so," she said, still with sleep in her eyes, but much more coherent than before. "Thanks, George," she said as she walked into the darkness of her house.

My father woke me up the next morning. As the world came into focus, I saw my mother standing next to him, a few steps behind. Her eyes were red. "George," my father said to me in the same stoic manner he said most everything. "There's something that I have to tell you. Something important. Do you need another minute? I let you sleep as long as I could." He put his hand on my shoulder.

"No. What is it?"

"It's Arthur."

"Arthur?"

"He was in a car accident last night." Adrenaline shot through me and I sat up quickly and got out of bed.

"Is he okay?"

"Oh, George," my mother said breaking into tears.

"He died, George."

Emotion left me completely. "What happened?"

"He was driving home last night and lost control of his car. He swerved off of the road and ran into some trees. There was a girl in the car with him. But she's okay. One of the trees was closer to the road than the one next to it and took most of the impact."

"It's okay to be sad, George," my mother said after wiping her eyes with back of her hand and wrapping her arms around me as she began to sob again.

"I know." I was still numb. "I need to get out of the house," I said, pulling away. And quickly pulling on a pair of jeans and a t-shirt.

"George," my dad said to me as I put on my shoes.

"I'm not going to drive." He nodded back.

You're gonna be cold," my mom said behind me as I rushed down the stairs and out of the front door.

Liberty's house was about a mile from mine. As I approached it, my chest heaving, ten or so cars lined either side of the street. The large picture window that sat centered on the front of the house was filled almost completely with other students. The Liberty that they had come to support, wasn't the person I wanted desperately to see. To hold. To cry with. I turned around and walked slowly home.

A few hours later I heard a knock on my bedroom door. "Yeah," I said focusing still on the video game I had been playing.

"Hey, George," a familiar, yet surprising voice said. I paused the game and turned my head. Franklin Paz was standing in the doorway.

"Uh. Hey, Franklin," I said shocked. "What's up, man?" Franklin had never been to my house. Franklin and I had never been friends. At least not really. He was two grades behind me and played the tuba in the band. He was so short and so round that most of the time it seemed like the tuba was playing him, producing all of the grunts that left his closed mouth as he attempted to keep the instrument steady. He was a terrible musician. He was tone deaf and had the rhythm of schizophrenic gerbil. And he was terribly annoying. You know that one kid that asks ridiculous and frequent questions that drive not only the teacher, but everyone else nuts? That was Franklin. Somewhere along the line he got it in his head that we were friends, even though I wanted nothing to do with him. If he saw me on campus he would waddle over to me as fast as he could and start rapid-firing at me. When I shooed him away, which was pretty much every time, he always went, and never seemed to be taken aback by it, always at my heels again the next time he saw me.

"Hey, George," he said again. "I…uh…I know you were really close with Arthur. And I heard what happened. So…I thought I would come and see how you were doing…man."

"I don't know." He still stood awkwardly in my doorway. "Do you play?" I asked, gesturing to the game paused on my television screen.

"Well, not that one. I've never played that one. But I can—I mean I'll try."

"Here," I unraveled and reached out the second controller. Surprisingly he took it without saying a word, took a seat on the floor and played Guardian Heroes with me. We played for about an hour with only the sounds of the game vibrating in the air.

After checking his watch, he abruptly stood up, which took longer than it would have for most everyone else, but was quick for him. "I gotta go," he said as he began to wrap the controller cord around. "I've got to watch my little sister."

"Don't worry about that," I said, taking it out of his hands.

"Oh. Okay. Thanks, George."

"Sure."

"Hey, George," he said as he reached the threshold of my room.

"Yeah."

"I'm really sorry."

"Thanks, man." He just smiled and then turned to leave. "Hey, Franklin."

"Yeah," he said turning back around.

"Thanks for keeping me company."

"Sure thing...man."

"I'll see you at school."

"Okay, yeah. At school. Bye George," he said as he bounded slowly down the stairs.

He was a better friend than I had ever given him credit for.

Arthur's funeral was three days later. I still hadn't seen Liberty. I called once, but her mother said that she wasn't available. My mom was friends with Mrs. Scott and she had spoken to her a few times. She told me that Liberty wasn't really talking to anyone. She barely left her room.

It seemed like the entire town was at the large Baptist church that Arthur's grandmother had been going to since she was a child. I sat with my parents about ten rows back. I could see Liberty on the front row with her parents next to Ida May. The service lasted about forty-five minutes. Then everyone left the church and drove over to the cemetery on the other side of town. Not the cemetery next to Thompkins park. A different one. A newer one.

Dark clouds filled the sky as if Pensdale herself was mourning. I stood with my parents and watched Arthur's casket get lowered slowly into the ground. Tears fell from my cheeks. I held my jaw tight, refusing to let everything out. It was still so surreal. Even as I took a shovel of Georgia red clay and tossed it on top of the shining black casket, I still couldn't believe that Arthur was gone. Liberty had been the first to be handed the shovel. She quickly poured a small scoop of ground into the rectangular hole and then pushed her way through the crowd. After my turn, I searched for her, walking quickly in the direction she had less than a minute earlier.

I saw her. She was sitting underneath a large oak about a hundred feet away from Arthur. I closed the space between us. She didn't see me at first. Her head was down and she had a metal nail file in her right hand. She was furiously scraping off the dark blue nail polish on her left hand. "Liberty," I said as a drop of rain hit my shoulder. She looked up. For a moment we just stared at each other as more drops fell from the sky at an accelerating pace. Then she looked back at her hand.

"I just can't, George. Please go."

"You can't what? I don't understand. Why?"

She stood up as the rain fell fiercely on both of us. "It hurts too much. Seeing you hurts too much. I just can't take it." The rain pounded on her face as she spoke and the foundation she had been wearing washed off in streaks, leaving behind the freckles on her face that had been muted for years like stars behind a layer of smog. "I'm leaving."

"Where are you going?"

"To stay with my aunt."

"Where?"

"Far away from here."

"Can I—"

"Let me go, George. Please let me go."

I stood there in the rain and watched her walk away, numb with loss. The wetness that covered me the only thing making me feel that I was alive at all. I noticed at the base of the tree something white as I turned away from the last time I would ever see Liberty. A crumpled piece of notebook paper. I picked it up and put it in my pocket. It was wet, but the leaves above had kept it dry enough to not fall apart.

ONE DIRTY TABLE

I found my parents in our car after a slow walk back to the parking lot. As we drove home I pulled the paper from my pocket and opened it. It was a poem.

And then night spoke raging in its melancholy of the promise of the light, if only to be silenced by the dawn.

CHAPTER NINETEEN

I was twelve. I had this dream. All of a sudden a countdown began from ten. As soon as it did, I was filled with horror. I was supposed to be somewhere. I was in some kind of command center or something, like you'd find at NASA. I raced out of the building as the countdown reverberated through me. In front of me was this multi-colored rocket that looked like it was made out of giant Legos. There was no doubt in my mind that I was supposed to be on it. I ran as hard as I could. As I ran and the countdown descended—I realized abruptly that I wouldn't make it. I stopped and watched the rocket take off with a roar. As I stood there I felt as though my skin had turned to glass and everything inside of me was gone.

  I never had that dream again, but it was always there in the back of my head—that feeling. That sense of loss. I thought I had it figured out though as I got older. That multi-colored rocket was my potential. I've never come close to reaching it. But now I'm not so sure. Maybe that rocket was my childhood. My innocence. Maybe it meant nothing. But ever since that morning, I've been looking for something to fill that void inside of me. Some days, even weeks, or months at a time, I don't notice it. But other days, days like today, it consumes me. Usually I just drink. But it never helped. It's funny looking back how sure I was that I had no doubt what could take that feeling away from me. Sometimes just being around Liberty was enough to make me forget. That one afternoon, when we sat underneath the big willow on the edge of that tiny pond and she put her head on my shoulder. That was perfect. I've been chasing that ever since. That moment. Even when everything crashed and fell apart around me, I clung to that feeling of holding her. I would save her. And that, was what would save me. But I didn't. And then she left.

And now, twenty years later, everything before college feels like a dream. And I find myself more often than not trying to filter out the reality of my life as a whole. But that's the problem. The truth most times is much more painful. It's a whole lot easier to pretend that the dream is real. Because once you recognize it and understand it to be nothing more than a dream, you can never go back. No matter how hard you try. I understand that now. My wanting to find Liberty has actually been the want to dream again. I have been so tired of feeling alone in the world. Everyone else sleepwalking around me.

I don't like to take walks. Even before I spent my evenings quickly pacing around tables and in and out of the kitchen, I didn't like them. But for the rest of the morning and into the early afternoon I wandered around my neighborhood. I brought my headphones with me, but never put them on. I found myself sitting in a swing at a park a few blocks away from home. At first I was alone, but after a few minutes a young mother and her son began to play on the jungle gym. He couldn't have been more than three or four. I watched him play. His mother watched intently as he climbed the wooden ramps that crisscrossed back and forth up to the top of the slide at the side of the jungle gym closest to me. Then she would go to the bottom to catch him. I must have watched this little kid, wearing green corduroy pants and an orange and blue plaid shirt, sit at the top of the slide twenty times. Each time he hesitated. He didn't seem scared, though. It was more like he just wasn't ready to go down yet. Like he was savoring the moment. He sat there with a puckish grin for at least a half a minute before he shoved off, squealing the whole way down and into his mother's arms.

I got to work early that night. The kitchen was bustling with prep and eighties metal, but the dining room was empty. Per the health department the tables couldn't be left set over night, at least not with silverware. There could be glasses, but they had to be turned upside down. I grabbed a handful of forks from the server station and began to place them down an inch above the edge of where the white linen fell off of the table and in line with the left edge of the chair behind it. Knives were on the right edge of the chair. Usually this was a process done by four or five people. At most, taking five minutes. With many other tasks to be accomplished before line up, the silverware was thrown down haphazardly—it was the responsibility of the server who had a particular table in their section to make sure that everything was precise. By the time the next server walked into the dining room I had finished all of the the knives and forks, and was beginning to place butter knives on the right edge of small bread and butter plates that sat to the left of each fork.

The night was slow. Only a handful of tables coming in. Usually we had five or six servers on a normal Tuesday, but tonight only four. Lineup was brief. Nothing on the a la carte or tasting menu had changed from the night before and we weren't out of anything. The four servers on the floor happened to be the four strongest in the staff. Jim knew this, so he didn't feel the need to go into any talking points of service. "You guys got this?" he said, looking each of us in the eye.

"Good. Chef's off tonight. No mistakes." he said quickly as he turned away from us and walked into his office. It was the shortest line up that I had ever had.

I didn't get the first table of the night—or the second, third, or fourth. You'd think that being one of four servers I'd at least get the fourth table, right? Nope. The front door was trying to be cute again. I did however get the fifth—a table of four women probably in their early fifties—and the sixth—four businessmen—loafers with no socks. I shoved down my frustration at being double-sat on one of the slowest night's we'd had in weeks and decided to just handle it.

I swung by the ladies first to drop off the menu and see if I could get a drink order. As I approached the table, one of the spacious booths towards the back of the dining room, the woman sitting in position four on the right side of the booth closest to me, cut me off as I opened my mouth to say hello. "I just want to make sure that you know that I have a gluten allergy." she said pointedly to me. "I absolutely can have no gluten."

"She's serious," the lady across from her said. "It's a very serious thing."

"Yes, ma'am. I—"

"And I'll have a Cosmo." the first woman said, cutting me off again. "But I don't want an orange in mine. I want a lime peel."

"Yes, ma'am. A lime peel." I said as I pulled my notepad out of my pocket and began to write the order down.

"And I'll have the same." said the woman who had driven home the whole gluten allergy thing. "But I want a cherry in mine as well as the lime."

"Yes, ma'am. A cherry." I said as I wrote while the thought that overwhelmed my head was that I needed to get to those businessmen before they got upset.

"I'd like a Cosmo, too," said the lady in position two, on the inside of the booth next to the cherry woman, "but I'd like it with the orange."

"Yes, ma'am," I said, "a classic cos—"

"But I want the bartender to put a dash—just one dash—of bitters in mine."

"Yes ma'am. One dash of bitters."

"And make sure that it is very cold. It has to be very cold." I didn't repeat that.

"I'd like a Cosmo as well." the fourth woman said, sitting to the inside of the gluten lady. "But I want mine on the rocks."

"Cosmo on the rocks. Very goo—"

"But I want the bartender to shake it first. Chill it, before pouring it on the rocks. It needs to be very cold."

"Mine needs to be very cold as well." the first two who ordered chimed in together as I turned from the table quickly saying that I would get their drinks started. As I turned I expected the table of businessmen to be looking around in frustration. But as I looked over I saw Trey walking away from them. He saw me hustling towards him and winked.

"I got you, bro." he said. "They want two bottles of Araujo. The main guy—seat two—he wants the first bottle poured out.

"Thanks, man." I responded quickly as I rushed to the computer to put in those ridiculous drinks. Araujo is over five hundred a bottle.

"I'll grab the wine." he said, walking the other direction.

I saw Mark by the host stand after double checking that the cocktails were all ordered correctly. I walked quickly over to him. "Hey, is there any way you can run drinks to table forty-two? I've got to get over to sixty and open some wine."

"Yeah, sure George." he said with a knowing smile and a quick look towards Catherine the hostess, knowing that I had been double sat for no reason.

"Thanks." I said as took off towards my other table.

"Glasses and trivets are down," Trey said as he handed me the two bottles of very expensive Napa Cab.

"Thanks, brother."

He nodded back.

I placed one of the bottles on a small round silver wine coaster, and then presented the other bottle to the guy who ordered it. I could tell immediately that he was the alpha at the table. He was the oldest by at least ten years. His hair was almost entirely gray and the Rolex on his left wrist probably cost more than most used cars. Plus, the man across from him was talking, but the other two suits on either side of him kept looking back at the older man every few seconds to see how he was reacting. "The Araujo two thousand and two," I said as I cradled the bottle in my left palm and supported the neck with my right hand.

"Yes. Thank you." he said after glancing at the bottle quickly. I opened the wine and poured him a taste. He picked up the large Bordeaux wine stem, swirled the wine and then smelled it. He then looked back towards me and nodded. As Trey had told me he requested, I poured out the bottle evenly into four glasses. I then opened the second bottle and poured another taste in the second glass that had been placed in front of the gentleman. He took a long sip from his full glass before picking up the second one and smelling the splash from the second bottle. He nodded again.

I waited a few seconds for a gap in the cadence of conversation before I interrupted. "Gentlemen," I said just as one of the younger men at the table finished a sentence, "would you like me to go over the menu today?" While I spoke to all off them, I looked squarely at the guy who ordered the wine.

"No need, sir." he said back to me quickly, but with a smile. I've been bragging all week about this place—about this spinalis steak you have—and that's what I'll have. Medium rare. And I'll start with the foie gras.

"Yes, sir. The spinalis, medium rare, and the foie gras. Very good."

Then clockwise around the table, as though they had been rehearsing it all day, the other three men at the table ordered the exact same thing.

"I'll have some bread sent over right away." I said before turning away from the table. I then walked quickly over to the table of ladies. "How are your cocktails?" I said as I approached. One of the four ladies—the one who wanted hers shaken and then on the rocks—acknowledged me and smiled; the other two ignored me while nodding their heads in agreement to whatever the gluten lady had just said. "Would you like me to go over the menu?" I said, abruptly cutting of the gluten lady as she began to speak again. I smiled as big as I could.

"Um, no. We know what we want." the gluten lady said looking directly at me with a touch of ire in her eyes for being interrupted.

"Wonderful. I'll start with you ma'am."

She picked up the menu and searched with her finger before finding what she was looking for. "She and I," she pointed with the same finger to the woman directly across from her, "are going to share the tomato salad. And there—"

"Absolutely no gluten. Yes ma'am. I've already spoken to the chef." I said as I interrupted her again.

"Good. And I'll have the spinalis steak."

"Yes ma'am. The spinalis steak. And how would you like that prepared?"

"Medium—no medium rare—I'd like it in between medium and medium rare."

"Yes ma'am. For you?" I said as look towards the woman across from her—the one sharing the salad.

"I'll have the halibut. But instead of the carrots can I have broccoli?"

"Yes ma'am. The halibut with broccoli instead of carrots. And for you ma'am?" I looked to the woman to her left.

"I'll have the scallops."

"The scallops. Very good."

"But I don't want the mushrooms. Can you leave those off?"

"Absolutely. No mushrooms. And for you, ma'am?" I said to the final woman at the table.

"I'll start with the mixed greens salad—she and I are going to share that," she said as she looked across from her to the woman who had just ordered, "and then I'm going to have the halibut."

"Yes ma'am. The halibut." I waited for her to speak up again and ask for something to be altered or substituted. But she didn't. "I have some bread brought out for the three of you." I turned quickly away and walked briskly over to the computer to ring in both of my orders. I rang in the businessmen's food first, intentionally, and then the ladies, but their split salads arrived before the other table's foie gras. My hope was that even though the salads would come out quick, that the suits would eat their first course faster than the chatty women so I could get their steaks going.

Unfortunately, they both finished at the same time. As I entered the kitchen with the empty plates from the suits table, I saw four half-eaten, half salads being scraped off and then dumped in the dish pit. After dropping off the ones in my hand I walked right over to the expo to fire the steaks for the businessmen. As I approached, I looked at the board—at the four hanging tickets in front of Mike, the sous chef who was expoing—and saw that they had both been fired. The ladies ticket was first. I kept walking and headed straight to the businessmen. They looked happy. They loved the foie. I poured a splash of wine in each glass and then walked back to the kitchen. I got along with Mike alright, but he had recently been bumped up to Sous. It had gone right to his head. I thought about asking him to send out the steaks first, but I knew it wouldn't help. I kept moving.

About fifteen minutes later I went back into the kitchen to see how far out the food was. The pass was empty. I looked at Mike whose eyes were burning holes into the back of the head of Joe at the grill. I looked at the grill and saw five raw steaks. I looked back at Mike. He didn't look at me. He kept his gaze focused on the grill as if he thought that staring at them so intensely would make them cook faster. "He didn't clean the grill." he said. "For the gluten allergy. When he realized it, he went to grab the grill brush. But guess what. It wasn't where it was supposed to be. MIS EN PLACE!" He shouted to the quiet kitchen. "Mise en place." He said quietly to himself after a deep breath through his nose. "He found it. But the steaks for both tables burnt while Joe here was fiddling around!"

My first thought was why he—ultimately responsible for the food that left the kitchen when Chef wasn't there—hadn't noticed that the steaks were unattended and had someone turn them or move them to a cooler part of the grill. But I knew that there was no point in bringing that up. It was what it was at this point.

"How long?"

"At least fifteen. Maybe twenty. I'm not sending out meat that hasn't rested."

I dashed out of the kitchen. The ladies were deep in conversation, their second round of cocktails almost half full. They were fine. I neared the businessmen. Their glasses were almost empty, but I didn't want to draw attention to the fact that their food was taking so long. The alpha was talking and the others listened intently. I turned quickly and went to find Jim to catch him up on what had happened. He told me to keep an eye on both tables, but to give them some space. If they were drinking and talking, they'd be fine. I gave it another five minutes and then went to make sure that both tables had drinks in front of them. The four women's were half full. The glasses of wine on my other table were nearly empty. I approached them and as I did the older man made eye contact. "I think we'll need one more bottle," he said. He didn't seem upset at all. I was relieved.

"Yes, sir. I'll be right ba—"

"Hey!" the younger man at the table who had been talking when I first approached the table said harshly. "How much longer?"

"I'm very sorry, sir. Let me go and check. My apologies." I said, all of the years of practicing keeping outwardly calm, needed in this moment to not lose my cool. I turned away to go and find Jim. As my left foot moved forward he spoke again.

"I mean, come one. It's been like thirty minutes. What? Did you forget to ring it in or something? How hard is it to write something down and then ring it in?" As he spoke my eyes drifted to the left, towards my other table. The gluten lady was eating a piece of bread.

Something fundamental inside of me snapped.

I spun around. "You want to know why your food is taking so long!" I said back with venom in every word. He looked back at me with shock on his face. "I'll tell you. Do you see that woman over there? The one with too much Botox eating that piece of bread? Well she told me—she insisted that she had a gluten allergy. As you can see, she's full of shit! Because she demanded that absolutely no gluten touch her food, the kitchen had to scrub half of the grill clean before cooking her food. And because of that your steaks were over cooked and they had to make new ones. Like I said before, I'm sorry." Those last two words were almost a growl. When they faded away the restaurant was filled only with the faint ambient music that was usually drowned out by the hum of conversation.

I looked at the guy in charge and met his gaze. He didn't seem shocked at all. It was almost as though he was holding back a smile. I nodded at him and then walked away. I untied my apron and wrapped it around the plastic-coated server book that held all of my receipts and cash. Jim was standing in the aisle. His face showed confusion, but his eyes were raging. "I can't tell you how sorry I am." I said to him. "I just can't do this anymore."

"George…" His baritone voice followed behind me as I walked towards the front of the building. But I didn't stop. I pushed open the front door of the restaurant and stepped into the Georgia humidity that still lingered from the day. The graveled employee parking lot was behind the restaurant. The small, gray rocks crunched beneath my feet as I slowly approached my car. I sat in the ripped tan leather driver's seat, the door still hanging open, and closed my eyes. I breathed deeply, pausing for a few seconds after each exhale. After the longest minute of my life, I opened my eyes again, closed the door, turned the key in the ignition, and pulled out onto the street.

I drove. The sound of wind whipping through the window keeping the thoughts in my head company. Not angry thoughts. Or sad ones. Rather I thought about how I had gotten here. To this very place in time. Thoughts of acceptance. Realizing that I had never really believed I would find her. That my pursuit of Liberty was futile. That just like them, I still needed something to hold on to. I felt both alone and a part of everyone. And so I drove on into the night—east—towards the ocean. To that place of awe and humility that flows and crashes, pushes and pulls, and in the depths of darkness holds on to rippled stars.

I thought about Arthur. I thought, that in a way, the spark of our generation died with him. The children of the eighties, raised on grunge and hip-hop before their voices were gagged with political correctness. What did we stand for? What did we become? We let ourselves get sucked into the internet and then spit back out with no memory of dissidence or revolution. Whatever honesty we held onto in our youth—the sons and daughters of dreamers—melted away and ran into the sewers, washing away with it any innocence that remained. Now we are in our forties—bartenders—watching, listening with apathetic enthusiasm to the rest of the masses, having convinced themselves they have already won. Living out our lives in minor keys, our dark gaze pulled towards the horizon, waiting for the sun.

The End